CHEESE RUSTLERS

CHEESE RUNNERS TRILOGY
BOOK TWO

BY
CHRIS A. JACKSON

ISBN 1939837138
ISBN-13 978-1939837134

Cover art by Brian King
© Jaxbooks Publishing

Acknowledgements

Thanks so much to Bryan King for the cover art and to Charles Crawford for the cover concept. Special thanks to Jeff Breslauer for the idea to produce the story as an audiobook, and for bringing my characters to life with his great voice work.

CHAPTER ONE

DUMPED

Record # KR29387/β. Transcript begins:

I was looking over the rim of my fifth frozen margarita when a screaming man plummeted past the window of the bar.

The bar was on the 200th floor.

Normally such an occurrence would have raised a few eyebrows, or even spurred a phone call or two to the unfortunate people whose job it is to scrape plummeting people from the sidewalk. Not here. Everybody just kept sipping their drinks, staring out the windows or chatting with their drinking companions. Everyone except the guy beside me, who was passed out facedown in a bowl of spicy peanuts.

I took another sip and let it sit on my tongue for a bit, savoring the flavors of lime and tequila. Good, but not as good as Laila's.

Laila... Damn...

You see, we were on the top floor of the Bungee Tower, in Minneapolis. Part of the reason they put a bar on the top floor, I guess, is that most heavy drinkers can get a little vicarious satisfaction from watching people plummet past the windows to a less-than-certain fate.

Take the elastic cords off their ankles and it would have been closer to how I felt.

I sipped again. I was feeling a little woozy and all the show tunes I'd ever heard were starting to play in my head.

I resisted the urge to break into song.

I sipped again as another screaming tourist fell past. I started to involuntarily hum the theme from The Sound of Music.

1

Yep, the drinks were getting to me.

Not the alcohol, of course, but the cold. I get brain freeze pretty bad, even though I don't have a brain to freeze. Well, not a *real* brain, anyway.

Sometimes I wish I could *really* get drunk.

I mean, when normal men—men without prosthetic cybernetic brains, that is—get dumped by their girlfriends, what do they do? They go out and get rip-roaring drunk! It's a rite of getting dumped. You drink to forget that you're the dumpee, and to justify the stupid things that come out of your mouth; things that you have utterly no control over, drunk or sober, I might add, most of which concern why *you* dumped *her*.

Yeah, I got dumped.

I know what you're going to say: "She seemed like such a nice clone..." Yeah, that's what I thought, too.

I sipped again.

"The hills are alive..." I murmured, out of key. I can sing about as well as a Turpenoid plays ice hockey, so it was probably a good thing that my bar companion was too busy trying to breathe peanuts to notice.

Oh, sure, *he* was drunk, the lucky sot! *He* could forget. *He* could sit there, obliviously drooling face down in a bowl of spicy peanuts!

"...with the sound of—"

A hand roughly the size of an Easter ham enveloped my shoulder and lifted me off my barstool.

I would have jumped, but my reflexes weren't working that well. I was wondering if my singing had disturbed someone after all, when Turk's voice tore through the haze of brain freeze.

"Come on, Harry! The *Limburger's* chirpin' like a hen with too many chicks! You've got more than a dozen messages and we can't read 'em!"

"Of course you can't. I changed all my passwords." He put me down and asked the obvious question with his eyes. I didn't want to wait around for the one or two neurons he possessed to click together and put his mouth into motion, so I answered. "I don't want you all reading Laila's letters. I mean, the poor girl's already got a broken heart. There's no reason to embarrass her, too."

"Not *those* messages. Zook broke into those files days ago. She just sent your letters back unanswered. But don't worry; only the bridge crew knows that Laila won't read your mail."

I stood and stared at him for a minute until I got a crick in my neck from looking up.

"Sorry she dumped you."

That was Turk's idea of sympathy. I took it with the intent in mind and decided it wasn't worth getting mad about. Turk had more exes than a Xexxian phone book, and Kik had left a trail of broken hearts—and other analogous internal organs, since many of the recipients of her xenophilic attentions didn't have hearts...eeew—halfway across the spiral arm. And Zook...well, Zook was an Immortal; who *knew* what he thought.

"Okay, I'll bite. What messages, then?"

"The encrypted ones. The board's got more red lights than Bourbon Street on a Saturday night."

That was Turk's second simile in less than five minutes. Either he'd been working on these all day, or he'd been renting brain space from someone.

"Laila's board?" *Laila's* board... Damn...

"Uh, yeah."

"Crap!"

"What?"

"Nothing." Well, obviously not, but I wasn't going to spew Company business around a place like this. Half the drunks in the place could have been Farfnian stooges. "Let's get back."

"Atta-boy, Harry!"

He slapped me on the back, almost putting me through the bar window. Almost was good since it was two hundred floors down and I was bungeeless. I rebounded off the inch-thick glass just as another screaming tourist plummeted past.

"And as far as the crew is concerned, *I* dumped *her*!" I snapped, perhaps with a bit too much verve, if the glares from the drunks at the bar were any indication. Evidently they hadn't bought it either. Okay, so I talked a little.

3

"Whatever you say, Harry," Turk said, dragging me toward the elevator. "Can we go now?"

"Fine." Like I could stop us.

When the doors opened I stepped past him and Turk ducked in behind me. The elevator groaned a bit at the punishment of the sudden addition of a hundred forty kilos of raw meat—that was just Turk—and the door closed. Turk may not be the brightest LED in the tail light, but he's big and good in a fight. He's dependable, meaning you can depend on him to always do the dumbest thing you can imagine, and he's a fair tactician when he's glued to his scanners and there aren't too many distractions, like chewing gum or someone shooting at us. The latter tends to happen occasionally. I don't expect multi-tasking from him, breathing and walking at the same time, for instance.

He pushed "P2" and we began to descend.

Have I ever mentioned that I hate glass elevators?

I don't know what possessed me to pick this particular bar, perhaps the symbolic imagery of plummeting people just outside the window or maybe just the margaritas.

Laila's margaritas... Damn...

A screaming body plummeted past our descending elevator.

I knew exactly how he felt. But he was going to bounce...

As we descended in silence, three more screaming tourists shot past at thirty-second intervals. As we got lower, we could see them bouncing up and down on their elastic tethers, faces red, mouths open and screaming. I wasn't feeling very well. I don't get drunk, but I do feel some of the less-than-pleasant effects of alcohol. Hurling, for instance.

Suffice to say that when we reached the parking level, I felt better. I did feel sorry for whatever cleaning robot serviced the elevators. I would have left it a tip, if robots cared about money or cleaning up the messes that intoxicated humans invariably leave behind.

"Jeez, Harry. Couldn't you wait until we got to the parking lot?"

"Sorry." I tiptoed out of the elevator and found a water fountain. When I was through, I found my security chief standing with his tree-trunk arms folded like a traffic barrier, his eyes scowling at me like two gun ports in a bunker. "Put yourself down for one day's hazardous duty pay, all right?"

Turk guided me to the car without a word.

"Gimme the keys."

He looked at me like I'd asked him for a kidney.

"Why?"

"Because I find it easier to drive when the car is actually turned *on*, Turk."

"Oh. I'll drive."

"No, I'll drive." I tried my I'm-your-boss-so-you-have-to-do-what-I-say look. It had all the effect of a bean on a bullet-train rail.

"You've been drinking, Harry. I'll drive." He reached for the door handle, but I put my hand against the door. Like I could have stopped him from opening it.

"I don't *get* drunk, Turk."

"What was that about, then?" He pointed back to the elevator, indicating my previous gastrointestinal distress. "You practicing for the Carpoolian puke choir?"

"That was a preview of coming attractions if I let you drive! Because the only thing more likely to make me sick than a glass elevator surrounded by bouncing tourists on elastic strings is you behind the wheel of this car. Besides, that was my gut, not my head." I tapped my forehead with a finger. "Prosthetic brain, remember?"

"I know that, Harry, but if we get stopped, the cops don't know it, and your blood alcohol's gotta be through the roof! You smell like a tequila factory!"

"If we get stopped, I'll dazzle them with feats of coordination and mental prowess. Now hand me the keys."

"Fine, Harry." He dropped them in my hand. "But I'm not bailing you out of the can again."

Okay, so it had happened *once* before. But I beat it in court. I drank a fifth of scotch during the hearing and did some simple calculus in my head for the judge while juggling wax fruit. It's not a bad party trick.

I opened the car door.

"Hey! You found him!"

Mishi's high-pitched voice nearly fractured my skull, but I managed to smile and nod. It did no good to bitch at the Turpenoid, it just made him more surly, which is like throwing gasoline on a...well...on a Turpenoid. His body temperature hovers just above that of boiling water, and his temper matches it perfectly. Fortunately, he was currently wearing a thermal "bunny" suit that was plugged into the van's utility socket, with only his four hands and face showing.

"What are you doing here, Mish?" The boarding ladder descended and I climbed into the vehicle, a full-sized Chrysler-Benz-Boing® Strato-Navigator™ deluxe SUG—Sport Utility Grav-vehicle. It had enough cargo space to fit two FZFG® teams.

What? Oh, Full-contact Zero-gee Frisbee™ Golf; it's replaced all other sports on Earth.

I adjusted the seat forward about a foot—Turk had been driving—secured the crash restraints and fired up the grav-turbines. Yeah...power...and a whole three miles to the gallon of deuterium! Oh, did I mention that they solved that pesky global warming thing?

"I brought lunch!" Mishi announced, unzipping his bulky garment and pulling out several foil-wrapped packets. "We figured you'd be drinking, so I thought you'd need some solid food and someone to talk to on the way back. No offense," he said to Turk, who made a practice of ignoring the Turpenoid.

"Besides," he continued, jerking a thumb at the back of the van, which was packed chuck-a-block full of food, "we did a little shopping."

"For the *Limburger*?" I glanced at Turk as I piloted the vehicle out of the parking garage and into the open air. I merged with traffic—I even used my blinkers, not wanting Turk to be proven right if we got pulled over—and asked, "Something you're not telling me?"

"Well, not really." He fidgeted, which was enough to tell me he wasn't telling me everything. "The crew's getting antsy, and the ban should be lifted soon. The patrols over The Barn have eased off, so we should be able to pick up our next shipment and take off. I just thought it'd be best if we were ready, you know."

I nodded and changed lanes. The Farfnians and their trained human search dogs had been sniffing around for months, but hadn't found anything, of course. The Wisconsin Cheese Company is *very* well hidden. Personnel could come and go without much trouble, but flying a stringship out of the side of a holographic barn with our Farfnian overlords watching like a flock of craboid vultures wasn't a good idea.

"Tired of paid vacation?"

"Not me!" Mishi quipped, unwrapping a sandwich of braised lamb and onions on flat bread and handing it to me. We were on the freeway, so I stabbed the cruise control and took my lunch in hand, promptly burning my fingers. I took a bite and remembered why I put up with Mishi's caustic mannerisms.

"But then, I didn't just get dumped by my girl!"

Case in point.

"Can that, Mish!" Turk snapped around a mouthful of sandwich.

"It's okay," I lied, managing not to cough up the bite I'd just swallowed. "So you all thought that getting back to work would take my mind off my troubles, huh?"

"Nah! We just wanna make another haul. Though, now that you mention it, Laila running off with that genetic engineer guy has slowed you down a bit."

"Uh-huh." I took another bite and chewed carefully.

"Can't imagine what a blow it was, her dumpin' you like that! Musta been a real twist of the knife that you had just paid for her new genome. Ha!"

"Actually, I'd been trying to forget that part. Thanks, Mish." That I had just paid everything I'd earned on our last trip to have Laila's cloned genome redesigned to mask her artificial nature had indeed been hard to swallow. I swallowed—not metaphorically— and my stomach decided to accept the proposition. Good stomach... Her running off with the guy who'd just done her gene-job—and what felt like a well-chosen pound of my flesh—had been the icing on the cake.

7

"Oh, don't mention it!" Mishi quipped. I don't think Turpenoids ever developed the concept of tact. Or if they have, they're keeping it their own little secret.

I handed the rest of my sandwich to Turk, who disposed of it in two bites without chewing more than four times in all. I glanced at him and saw something that might have been sympathy, but was probably indigestion.

Mishi continued yammering, but I won't go into details. The subject drifted away from my failed love life, which was merciful in and of itself. I contented myself with watching the cityscape devolve into suburb, and finally to patchy rural burgs tied together only by old surface roads that crisscrossed the landscape like lines on an old-fashioned printed circuit.

"Exit's coming up," Turk said, breaking my reverie and nodding to the dash.

"Yeah." I took the controls back and steered us down out of the stream of traffic into the slower lanes that hugged the old black-top roads of a miniscule town, the name of which escapes me. After a while we took a turn that led us out into an even more rural area. Mishi shut up, finally, just as we turned onto the old dirt road to Cowboy Bob's Emu Ranch.

Don't laugh. With cows declared illegal by our Farfnian overlords, emus had grown in popularity for several reasons. They're evidently easy to ranch, grow fast, taste good, and are ugly enough that animal-rights activists don't mind the rest of us eating them.

I waved out the window to Cowboy Bob—Yes, his name is really Bob. Why is that funny?—as we drove past the house and into his old garage. Wisconsin Cheese pays Bob a tidy sum for the use of his garage, which keeps him in emus, I guess. The SUG settled to the ground and I nodded to Turk, who took out his remote and punched in the proper code.

The floor lowered us down into the tunnel without a sound. This was just one of the secret ways in and out of The Barn. The tram we were lowered into was fully automated, so we just sat there as we were scanned, video recorded, and sniffed for any trace of Farfnian. We were clean, of course. If we hadn't been, I wouldn't be sitting here, since there are enough explosives wired to the scanners to leave nothing but a crater. I guess Bob might not be getting something for nothing after all. Anyway, there was only a short wait before the tram kicked into motion and we were whisked through the dark tunnel toward home.

Home...

I live underground, at least when I'm not flying through space or sitting on some alien planet. It's a nice place, and we can walk around the underground pastures and pat the cows all we want. Cows like that, which is Rule Number Two of the WCC: keep the cows happy. Wisconsin Cheese Company is completely underground and encompasses about a hundred multi-level acres of pasture, dairy, housing, and hangers for the forty or so cheese-smuggling stringships that distribute our product throughout the galaxy. We're the biggest cheese producer on the planet that I know of, and we live every minute with the knowledge that if the Farfnians found out about our little subterranean operation, we would shortly be visited by an asteroid the size of a football stadium. Which brings us to Rule Number One of the WCC, which is basically "Keep your (expletive deleted) mouth shut!" The slightest leak could bring that asteroid down, so we all tend to be pretty tight-lipped.

Did I mention that the Farfnians pretty much rule most of the galaxy?

Did I also mention that they don't tend to quibble about exterminating aliens—human or otherwise—to keep their hold on *their* galaxy?

Did I also mention that I love my job and wouldn't live anywhere else on Earth?

So, when the tram dumped us out into one of the production facilities and the heady scent of a dairy in full production mode wafted through the vents into the cab, I took a deep breath and smiled. I opened the windows and let that beautiful aroma fill my senses.

Yeah, home was good.

You don't like the smell of cows? You sure you're human?

I headed for one of the lifts and took it right to the top. The lift doors opened, and the wonderful aroma of cows and, well, cow stuff, was replaced with that of lubricant, ozone, jet fuel and scorched metal. The lifts are vented so this stench doesn't disturb our bovine benefactors, but I have grown enamored with this odor, too. It smelled like my ship, the *Limburger*, which also smelled like home.

I found her without any trouble. She had just received a major refit and was as shiny as a new penny. What's a penny? Oh, sorry, it's a coin that used to be worth one one-hundredth of a dollar. About as much as a ten-buck piece is worth now. Anyway, all her dents had been pounded out and she was buffed, polished, and had brand-new landing struts, since the old ones had been pretty beat up by Kik's last landing.

I didn't bother admiring her, but couldn't help feel a little tug of pride. Yeah, *my* ship... Did I tell you that I was Captain? No, really!

I stopped just short of the loading ramp and told Mishi to have the cargo handlers see to his provisions as Turk and I headed for the bridge.

"Are we leavin', Harry?"

"I don't know yet, Mish. But I wouldn't be surprised." I gave him the thumbs up as the door to the lift closed, and he returned a slightly different gesture, four of them in fact. Hmph...that's gratitude for you!

"Hey, Kik!" I snapped, entering the bridge from the lift. "Keep your feet off my chair!" She was lying on the deck throwing a beanbag at the overhead and catching it, her bare feet propped up on the captain's chair.

"Keep your ass off my foot rest!" She rolled to her feet and threw the beanbag at me. "It's about time you got back! We gettin' out of here?"

"Don't know." I rubbed the spot where the bag had hit and sat down at the communications console. No, it is not *Laila's* chair, damn it! There were, indeed, about fifteen red lights blinking on the display. I touched the first, decrypted it and cringed. It was a day old, and marked "URGENT".

Oops!

I skimmed the comment and cringed again. Then checked my watch. Then cringed one more time for good measure.

"We're late," I said, toggling through the rest of the messages to confirm that they were just the same message repeated, each marked more urgent than the last... Yep. *Damn.*

"Late for what?"

"A senior-officer's meeting at WCC Central. It started ten minutes ago."

"All those messages were just calling you to a stinking meeting?"

"My guess is that it's a rather *important* meeting, Turk. They could have told us to load up and make our run any time." I keyed open the ship intercom and said, "Zook, drop whatever you're doing and meet me in the loading bay."

"Sure, Harry!" I heard a clank in the background before the comm went dead. He's so literal! I hoped whatever he dropped wasn't fragile or expensive or both.

"Senior officers. Does that mean all of us?"

"Yes, Kik. You'll have to put your shoes on."

"Try this on for size."

She made the same gesture that my cook had so recently employed, but with only one hand. The other was reaching for a boot, so I let it slide. Kik had been pretty surly since Riffy, the Shesharrian ambassador and her latest interplanetary conquest, left for home.

Jeez... Some people just can't take getting dumped.

CHAPTER TWO

RUSTLED

The drive to WCC Central was very quiet, and not just because Mishi wasn't in the car. You'd think two people with something in common would get along, but Kik and I had been at each other's throats since we'd both been dumped. I was tired of it, but not tired enough to let her get in the last dig.

I'm such a grownup about these things.

By the time we arrived, the meeting was well underway, captains and executive officers of forty crews jammed into the meeting hall like sardines in a huge elliptical can. The tiers of seats were all full and several people were standing, so we just took up station near one of the exits.

"Meredith!" I stage-whispered to one of the other captains. "What have we missed?"

Meredith Grendler is a hard woman—Don't believe me? Try calling her Meri, but be prepared to duck—and a damn fine captain. She rules her crew with an iron fist. Well, it's actually titanium, composite, and a lot of gears and computer-neural interfaces. She lost the original in a firefight with a Farfnian hit team, and the replacement is a work of modern art and science. She glared at me, then decided that my interruption wasn't a smack-worthy offense and leaned close.

"They hit Tillamook."

My insides went cold.

By "they" she undoubtedly meant the Farfnians. By "hit" I assumed she meant that they'd dropped a very large rock from space. And by "Tillamook" I knew she meant the picturesque little town in western Oregon that was one of our fiercest competitors.

They couldn't produce our volume, but a block of Tillamook cheddar can send a Farfnian mud puppy into catatonic convulsions. They make *good* cheese.

Made good cheese.

"Holy crapoly!" My usual eloquence was making itself known.

I glanced at the grim three-dee images the Chief Exec was playing for the crowd. Most were nothing but views of a huge hole in the ground, all that was left of the Tillamook Cheese Factory. As the images flicked past, I filled in my crew on the details.

"The crabs must have found out where they were and dropped one on them," I finished. "Security's going to tighten up around here, or I'm a Carpoolian proctologist."

"It wasn't an asteroid, Harry." That was Zook, and his comment got the attention of everyone within ten feet, which was quite a few people since we were standing as close as groupies in a tour bus.

"What was it then, a two-million-ton Twinkie®?"

Sometimes I wish Turk would give up trying to be funny.

"There's no ejecta, and the surrounding strata show no signs of compression wave fractures."

"Some new kind of Farfnian beam weapon?" Meredith asked, her tone dangerous.

"The Farfnians didn't do it."

"Huh?" That was me... Yeah, Mr. Eloquent was back, all right.

"What are you talking about, Zook? Of course it was the Farfnians!" Kik pointed at the graphic image of a half-kilometer-wide crater in three-dimensional color right there for everyone to see. "If they didn't, then who blasted Tillamook to smithereens?"

"No one."

"Huh?" Wow, two in a row. I was on a roll.

"What the hell was it then, a very large sink hole?"

"Kik, I don't think—"

"Then don't open your mouth, Turk! Zook's out of his mind, and I'm not going to stand here and listen to it!" She turned and started to storm off.

"Tillamook wasn't hit; it was stolen."

That got everyone's attention, and brought Kik back like a package without enough postage. It caught me so far off guard that I couldn't even manage another "Huh?" and made enough commotion from the surrounding crews that the uproar finally caught the attention of the Chief Exec.

"If the crew of the *Limburger* would kindly shut the hell up, we've got work to do here!"

The entire hall went silent. You could have heard a security officer's stomach rumbling from ten feet away; Turk's lunch evidently wasn't settling very well. Then a voice cut through the silence, and that it was mine left me utterly flabbergasted!

Interesting word, that. Did you know it actually comes from the words flabby and aghast? Well, I guess that *does* kind of describe me, but... Oh. Sorry. I digress. Well, the voice surprised me, because it was mine.

"Sorry, Chief, but my engineer, Zook here, says that Tillamook wasn't hit by the crabs." That got a few murmurs of disbelief. "He says it was stolen." That got quite a few more murmurs and a number of expletives relating to the excrement of male bovines.

I was used to the abuse. Having a smart-ass bridge crew has its advantages, I guess.

"*Zook* says?" The Chief glared, his forehead wrinkling into rows of parallel lines. "He's one of *those*, isn't he?"

Not everyone knew Zook was an Immortal. It wasn't exactly a secret, but it wasn't something we talked about either. Some people don't *like* Immortals, and the dislike in the Chief's voice was as plain as the nose between his beady little eyes.

I did not cringe, I did not make a face, and I was not violently ill. It took a lot of effort, but I didn't do these things. I don't particularly like it when people make judgments on other people with respect to gender, race, sexual preference, religion, or species. I've even met *Farfnians* I liked, so I try to keep an open mind. But calling the CEO what I felt like calling him would only earn me trouble, so I tried to keep the sarcasm out of my voice when I said, "Which *those* are those, sir?"

"You know perfectly well what I mean, Captain Fische."

"I am an Immortal, sir," Zook piped up, utterly fearless—or maybe oblivious—with regard to the fallout such an admission might elicit. "And it is obvious that this wasn't the Farfnians."

"Well, ENN™ has been reporting on it all day, and the Farfnians have taken full responsibility!"

In case you're not from Earth, ENN™ is Earth News Network. It's the only Farfnian-approved "liberal-media" network, and so the only legal news broadcast world-wide. We in the cheese-smuggling business tend to doubt the level of veracity of the broadcast, and some have even gone as far to say that it is tainted, nay, even swayed by the mega-billion farf donations that keep the network on top of the ratings list. Yeah, that's right. Tainted.

I checked the bottom of my boots just in case I had stepped in any *taint* when I crossed the cow pasture.

Okay, so I'm a little cynical with regard to ENN™ broadcasts.

"Exactly!" Zook said with a smile.

"Huh?" That was actually the CEO, not me, though I was thinking it.

"Why would they not claim they'd done it? It is a victory in their War on Cheese. They will put it on every holovid on the planet!"

"Oh, so it's obviously much more plausible that some invisible entity scooped up a cubic mile of earth and snuck off with it?" The CEO's sarcasm, at least, was in full form.

"Why, yes," Zook said, with that innocent genius smile of his.

"This is ridiculous! The Farfnians did this and we're next if we don't tighten down security! I'm putting a full lockdown in force as of right now! Nobody goes in or out, and we minimize our signature; I want zero EM and BM output!"

That's Electromagnetic and Bovine Methane, in case you didn't know. The crabs have sniffers all over the planet trying to detect cow farts. Methane emissions have been the doom of more than one secret cheese-production facility.

There was some grumbling, but I wasn't expecting Kik to step out in front of me and shout down at the CEO like a jilted bride from a second-floor church window.

"Are you losing your (expletive deleted) mind?" At this point I must admit that she was not exuding her usual aura of holy-cow-would-you-look-at-that-babe-ness. Maybe she turned it off for the occasion. "If Zook's right, and someone's stolen Tillamook, then they can start their own cheese production!"

That got a few murmurs, both in agreement and bordering on obscene.

"We've got to find out where they've taken it, and get it back!"

"Now that's just about enough!" the CEO roared. Well, maybe he just said it loudly, but the amplifiers that let us all hear him made it a roar. "Captain Fische, control your pilot!"

"That'd be a first," Turk said with a smirk.

I hated to agree, but it was true. And "if you can't beat 'em, join 'em" has always been an axiom I attempt to live by, so...

"I'm on her side, Chief," I said, almost scaring myself out of my meager lunch. "And if Zook says it wasn't the crabs, that's good enough for me!"

"Well, not for me! And I make the decisions around here!" The Chief made a gesture and the house lights went up, obliterating the three-dee slide show. "The lockdown starts right now! Everyone back to your ships! This meeting's over!"

"You absolute—"

"Wait, Kik!" I grabbed her arm before she could push through the crowd and do someone bodily harm. "Listen for a second!"

She stopped and glared back at me, then looked down at my hand on her arm with an expression that clearly said I was about to lose my fingers if I didn't remove it.

"Let go of me, Harry!"

"No, I won't. I need you to pilo—"

I would have finished the sentence, but that was when Kik's fist hit me square in the nose.

I managed not to let go of her arm, but something in my head went *click*, and the next thing I knew, my mouth was saying something. And not just saying it, but *singing* it...

"I'm a Yankee Doodle Dandy, Yankee Doodle do or die!" I brayed in my worst James Cagney imitation. I tried to stop, but there was something whirring through my mind that wouldn't let go. It was like I was possessed by a five-foot four-inch Republican or something!

Then Zook rapped me hard just over my left ear, and everything was back to normal.

"What the hell was that, Harry?" Kik asked, chuckling to herself.

"Beats the hell out of me," I said, hoping she wouldn't take it as a suggestion. I rubbed my nose. It hurt. "Just don't hit me again, okay?"

"Just don't grab me again."

"Then stop and think, Kik, and the rest of you, too." That got their attention well enough for me to drop the little bombshell that had been percolating in my mind for the last few weeks. "We can leave any time we want, lockdown or no, and without a single Farfnian patrol spotting us."

"What?"

"How?"

"By shifting the ship into stringspace," Zook said with a grin that told me he was already working on the equations in his head.

"You mean in the *hanger*?" It's amazing that someone as big as Turk can hit such a high note when he's terrified.

"Position is irrelevant in stringspace, Turk," Zook explained, which did nothing to return any color to my security officer's face.

"But how do we get back this time?" Kik asked, hands on hips and once again radiating enough hottiness to bake a cake. "You going to take another walk outside the ship?"

"Leave that to me," I said with my best I-am-a-higher-being smile. "Let's get back to the ship!"

I let Kik drive back while I sat shotgun and made a few calls. Yes, I *can* multi-task, but talking on the phone and driving is one of my pet peeves. By the time we arrived, the cargo handlers were loading our standard load: two metric tons of Wisconsin's highest quality cheddar, vacuum-sealed and ready for concealment in our secret hold. I got out of the van and plugged my nose, because they were just starting to load the decoy cargo, and rotten calamari is even worse than sardines.

"Give me a thumbs up when you've got that locked down and the hold fumigated, okay, Charley?"

"Sure, Harry," my chief cargo handler said, his voice muffled from behind his gas mask.

"So, Zook," I said as the lift doors closed, "can we really do this inside the hanger, or are we just going to make a crater the size of the one where Tillamook used to be?"

"You mean you don't *know*?" I was thinking Turk would make a good soprano if I could just keep him terrified.

"We can do it, Harry, but I am a little worried about the proximity of other solid objects when we do." He smiled innocently, which is never good. "We could take a sizable piece of real estate with us."

"There are four other stringships parked next to us, Zook. Taking parts of them with us would be a bad thing."

"The problem is," he said, wagging a finger in a very professor-like manner as we exited the lift onto the bridge, "that the tangent of the spheroid graviton wavelength is not cohesive within parameters that exclude diametrically opposed particle-charge variances."

"Uh, yeah. I knew that." I had no idea what he was talking about.

"Then you understand that I need Kik to hover the ship."

"Well, of course!" Still clueless. "Uh, how high?"

"About twelve meters, I think, ought to do it."

"No problem. Go ahead and do what you have to do at your console, Zook. Kik and I need to discuss something."

When Zook was out of earshot, I looked at Kik imploringly. She knew I wasn't much of a techie.

"He means that the jump field is a sphere, but he can smoosh it enough out of shape to keep from shearing off pieces of anyone else's hulls if I hover halfway between the roof and the floor."

Damn, she's sexy when she translates gibberish into something I can understand.

"Yeah, that's what I thought he said."

She smirked at me, but I let it go. At least we weren't at each other's throats for a while.

"I've only got one question, Harry," Turk asked, collapsing into his crash couch like a half-ton steer in a slaughterhouse.

I should be so lucky. Turk never had just *one* question.

"What the hell are we doing?"

"We're leaving, Turk." He looked at me blankly. Well, okay, even more blankly than he always looks. "You know, *lee-ving*." Sometimes it helps if I talk slowly and enunciate. "The opposite of staying?"

"I *know* that, Harry!" he growled, his face flushing that shade of mauve that either means he's embarrassed or about to rearrange my skeletal structure. I sincerely hoped it was the former. "I mean, where are we going and what do we plan to do when we get there? Start asking 'Hey, you know anyone who might have stolen Tillamook? It's about yea big and kinda smells like cows.'"

He spread his arms to indicate the size of Tillamook. The scary thing was that he was closer than you might think. Not just with the size thing, but with his estimate of my plan. Funny, it sounded better when it was in my head.

"No, we won't just start asking strangers, Turk. We'll ask friends. That's what the cheese is for. We need something to barter information with."

"Preposition, Harry." Kik said.

"Huh?"

"Preposition. You left your preposition dangling."

I looked down, but my fly wasn't unzipped. "Huh?"

"Your English sucks. You don't end a sentence with 'with'. It should be 'We need something to barter with *for* information.'"

Okay, I hate people telling me how to speak almost as much as I hate glass elevators.

"How about this: 'We need something to barter information with, Bitch!'"

She said something caustic, and I returned the favor. Pretty soon we were in a having a complete knock-down, drag-out hissy-fit at one another, which might have continued well into the next drink you buy me—(extended pause terminated with the sound of ice and scotch filling a glass)—except for Turk, who stepped between us

19

and yelled, "SHUT UP!" loud enough to peel the wax off my eardrums.

"You still haven't answered my question!"

"Oh, come on, Turk! How hard can it be to find a whole cheese factory, complete with cows and milking machines, that's been scraped out of the ground like a giant scoop of fudge ripple? It's kind of a hard item to sell on the black market! Every Carpoolian in the galaxy's got to be salivating buckets over this one."

"Besides, I know who stole Tillamook."

Kik, Turk and I stared at Zook as if he'd just turned green.

"Besides," I finished, sitting down and smiling my best all-is-well-with-the-world smile, "Zook knows who stole Tillamook."

"Rustled," Kik said, sounding a little subdued.

"Huh?" Hey, if something works for me, I stick with it!

"Rustled. When you steal cows, it's called rustling."

"What's it called when you steal cows, people, and entire dairy and several metric tons of high-quality cheese?"

"Cheese rustling." She sounded a little less numb.

"Then, that's your answer, Turk. We're going to go after them darn cheese rustlers, and bring back the...uh...herd, and all the rest of the stuff they stole." Okay, I even broke into a Texas drawl. I couldn't resist.

"So who stole it?" he asked Zook, taking me out of the loop and thus avoiding any more of my smart-ass comments. Hmph. There's loyalty for ya.

"Oh, well I'm pretty sure it was the S—" Zook made a sound like a cross between a toilet flush and cow flatus, both of which I'm pretty familiar with but am unable to produce with my vocal cords, so let's just call them the Sploig, shall we?

"The who?"

"The Sploig." He looked at us all like he'd just said something that made sense. "They're a race that disappeared about forty thousand years ago, just before the Farfnian's came to power. Some said they were beat by the crabs, but that's not true. They just vanished."

"Um, pardon my audacity, Zook, but if they vanished, how could they have stolen Tillamook?" Don't think that I really expected a straight answer. I was just curious.

"Well, obviously they used time travel."

"Well, of course they did!" Turk's mauveness was returning. "And I suppose they whisked Tillamook—cows, humans, cheese and all—right back to whenever they came from, just because they like the smell!"

"Well, I don't think so, Turk, but that could be the reason, I guess." He got one of those introspective looks that worry me more than Farfnian patrol cruisers.

"What were you thinking they would do with Tillamook, Zook?" It's best to get Zook back on track when he gets distracted, or he'll stay distracted for years, literally.

"Oh, well, I think they will probably dismantle it to figure out how cows make cheese, then take the secret back to a time before the Farfnians came to power and introduce cheese into their culture, thus arresting their development and causing their civilization to remain stagnant for millennia."

The rest of us blinked in amazement.

It made a scary kind of sense.

"Thus maintaining their dominance in the galaxy."

"And avoiding the whole vanishing thing," I put in.

"Precisely."

"And the whole intragalactic-war thing," Kik added.

"Uh, yes, if anyone ever was foolish enough to try to fight the Sploig."

"Well, if they were so powerful, why'd they vanish?" I hate to admit it, but Turk took the words right out of my mouth.

"Oh, well, I was being facetious. Nobody could *really* fight the Sploig, because nobody could ever find them."

"You mean after they vanished."

"No, before they vanished, too."

Now I was really confused.

Zook can do that to you.

"Let me get this straight. This race ruled the galaxy, but nobody could ever find them?" I asked, at the risk of being dragged deeper into the mire in which I was currently drowning. But a man sinking in quicksand will even grab a stone if it is thrown to him. Yeah, that's me, Mr. Philosophical.

"Exactly."

"Why not?

"Because they're shapeshifters, of course."

"Ahhh!" At least it's better than 'Huh?'

"So, they never really vanished, did they?" Kik asked, looking much less confused than me, which was irritating.

"Well, they stopped pressing their influence onto the other space-faring races, but no, I guess they *could* still be around." He looked from one of us to the other, his brown eyes squinting in sudden paranoid scrutiny. "Why, one could even be among us right now!"

"Stop that!" I snapped, popping him on the shoulder. "You're freakin' me out!"

A beep from my comm line interrupted the snickering Immortal, so I just glared and answered it. It was Charley. Everything was secure and ready.

"Okay, then. Everyone to your stations!" I said into the shipwide intercom. "We're going to be taking off, and it might get bumpy."

Turk went to his console and strapped himself in. Zook flopped into his seat, ignoring the restraints, since he considered being thrown around the bridge a mild amusement. Kik kicked off her boots and stripped, which I did *not* watch with bugging eyes and lolling tongue—okay, maybe I lolled a little—as I went to my locker and retrieved my emergency zero-gee rescue belt.

I strapped it on, grabbed a can of Jiffy Whip™, tested it to make sure it was full—yummy!—and put it in the holster. After our previous trip, I'd vowed never to be without a can of this stuff. It had, quite literally, saved our whipped topping!

Then I sat in my seat, plugged my head into the ship's computer—New toys! Wow! Cool!—and asked Kik, "You ready?"

"Firing her up now, Harry."

"Zook?"

"Everything's ready, Harry."

"Turk?" There was nothing for him to be watching, but he hates to be left out. And I hate to have my kneecaps shattered.

"Ready, Harry."

I looked at Laila's empty seat... *Damn*.

I punched up the communications panel myself and was elated to see the CEO's bulbous visage appear on the screen.

"What the *hell* do you think you're doing, Fische?" He was doing a fair imitation of Turk, as far as the color of his face went.

"I'm leaving, Chief."

"This facility is locked down, you moron!" he shouted incredulously, waving his arms in a poor attempt at either emphasis or flight. "The doors are closed! Just how far do you think you can get?"

"Um, about a hundred-and-thirty light years, I think." I was enjoying this much more than was good for my upward mobility within the company, but I couldn't help myself.

"The hell you are, Fische! Now shut your engines down, or I'll have your ship disabled!" He'd gone beyond mauve into a shade of puce that was very unattractive and rather startling.

"The main hanger guns are charging, Harry!"

Okay, maybe there was something for Turk to do after all. The landing-tunnel entrance is flanked by two very large ion cannons; large enough to punch a hole through my ship with one round.

Crap.

"Boss, we don't need you to open the doors for us to leave, and we're not going to attract the attention of the crabs. We'll be back, and we'll be bringing Tillamook back with us!" Brave words, but really stupid. They had the desired effect on the CEO, however. His face looked like someone had used his testicles for soccer practice just before I cut the connection.

"How long until they reach minimum firing power?" I asked, watching the engine temps rising through my computer link.

"About a minute. Maybe less."

"How long until we're airborne, Kik?" I asked on our private line.

"Any time, Harry. The mains aren't up to temp, but we don't need them in here. I can hover on atmospheric jets and maneuver with thrusters."

"Good. Do it! We're being rushed. The chief is charging the guns and doesn't want us to leave."

"We're up!"

The ship jumped up like a school teacher sitting on a tack.

"Zook?"

"The graviton field is shaping up, but I'll need a few seconds to get the shape right."

"How many seconds?"

"Thirty-seven."

At least he's precise. Double crap.

"Turk?"

"Less than that, I think." He looked at me, his jaw clenched like he was testing the strength of his fillings. "Do you really think he'll shoot us?"

"I wouldn't put it past him." I asked Kik, "Are the mains up to temp yet?"

"Barely, Harry. How much time?"

"Not enough."

"You want me to...?"

She didn't have to finish the thought. I knew what she was asking and I really didn't want to say yes, but...

"Do it, Kik!"

Now, I'm not one to try to make a dangerous situation worse, but I couldn't very well just sit there and wait for some nitwit to shoot me, could I?

Kik fired the forward thrusters, backed the ship right up to the nearest ion cannon and gave a love tap on the main engines. It was just enough to melt the projector array without shooting us across the hanger into the opposite wall.

"One down!" Turk yelled as we slewed over the parked ships and lined up for another puff. "It's too late, Harry! They're going to—"

"Kik!"

"I see it!"

She hit the mains on full just as the ion cannon fired. Now, those cannons pack a punch, but they don't measure up to a fusion drive at close range. The result was kind of like trying to pee against the stream of a fire hose. Unfortunately, while we didn't get shot, we did shoot right across the hanger. Kik tried to turn the ship, be we were going way too fast.

"Got it, Harry!"

I stared at Zook, wondering for half a second what he had gotten and if it was contagious; then I remembered.

"Stringspace, Kik!"

"Yeah!"

She sounded a little stressed, though I can't imagine why.

I had the viewer turned on and was watching the approaching wall right before everything disappeared into a sea of black with that peculiar little lurch that told me we were no longer in the real universe.

"Whew!" Turk was trying to rival my eloquence, and I just couldn't have that.

"Nice driving, Kik," I said, averting my eyes politely while she got out of the couch and into her jump suit. No, really, I did!

"Well, Harry," Zook asked, that evil boyish smile intact. It doesn't look evil, but I assure you, it is. "What is your plan for getting us back to the real universe?"

"Lunch."

"Lunch?" Turk looked at me, dumbfounded. My world was back to normal.

"Yes, lunch." Then I remembered that we ate in the van. "Second lunch, I guess."

"So, what's for lunch?" Kik was dressed...well, unless you count shoes.

"Turpenoid Surprise. My favorite dish!"

They all stared at me like I was crazy.

Yes, the last word is something to be cherished.

CHAPTER THREE

TURPENOID SURPRISE

Lunch was fantastic, as usual, which made me feel really terrible about the plan that had taken form in my head. Not bad enough to not go through with it, mind you, but bad nonetheless. I often wonder how my cybernetic prosthesis comes up with these things. I don't remember being this creative before having my brain downloaded onto Zook's palm computer.

I pushed back my chair and sipped my coffee, wondering, not for the first time, if I was the same person as before.

Maybe there was more different in me than being susceptible to brain-freeze and sudden jolts and the ability to do integral calculus in my head. Maybe this thing was turning me into some kind of evil, non-caring, plotting, cyborg monster.

Cool.

A license to party!

Well, okay, I knew I wasn't *evil*; I didn't kick puppies or squash butterflies, and bad things still bothered me, at least when they happened to good people. I can't say that I shed a tear when politicians get caught accepting bribes, or corporate big wigs get caught buying politicians.

Maybe everything that is Harry Fische was indeed downloaded onto that little computer that sits between the two halves of my dead brain, but I'd feel better if I *knew* I was still me.

"So, what's the plan, Harry?" Kik asked, interrupting my pensive moment. I don't have many of them, but I couldn't make myself get mad at her. She wasn't exactly smiling, but it wasn't the sneer I'd come to expect of late, either. Isn't it amazing how good food solves so many interpersonal problems?

"Well, I think we need to go to the galley for a few things, and if Zook can pick up one or two items from engineering, we'll be set."

"Let me guess," Zook said with that oh-so-innocent smile of his. "High temperature duct tape, a pair of long-handled tongs, a graviton emitter, and a blow torch." He sat there eying me like he already knew what I was planning, which he obviously did, since he just told me exactly what I was going to ask him to get.

The smug little twit!

Okay, Zook creeps me out. I love him, but he creeps me out. He just *knows* too much. Sure he's older than a few solar systems I've visited, but how does he keep all that crap in his head without exploding?

"Uh, yeah, that stuff and a six-inch coil spanner." I had absolutely no use for the wrench, except maybe to bonk him over the head with, but I couldn't let him think that he had me completely figured out.

"Okay. I'll meet you at the airlock."

"Fine." Yeah, creepy. I stood up and said, "Turk, Kik, I need you in the galley."

"What do we need from the galley?" Well, at least Turk didn't have me completely pegged yet. When that happens, I'm handing in my captain's license and taking up needlepoint as a career.

"Three pairs of pot holders and a fifty-quart colander."

"Harry, you're not going to—"

"Kik, what I'm going to do is get us back into the real universe and as far from Earth as I can. This is the only way I can think of, short of taking us straight to the Farfnian home world." I turned and did my best determined-captain stride toward the galley. "Since I don't think you want to go visit the crabs on their home turf in a ship full of controlled substance, I suggest you help me."

"Okay, but he's not going to like this."

"You think?"

I didn't need Zook to predict that.

"That lunch was great, Mishi!" I said, putting on my best happy-captain face as we entered the sweltering galley. It wasn't just hot in there, it was sauna hot, boiled-in-oil hot, and dip-me-in-picante-sauce-and-call-me-a-corn-chip hot all at once, which was just the way the king of this particular domain liked it.

Mishi didn't buy my 'happy captain' bit for a minute.

"What do you want, Harry? And why are you in *my* galley?" The suspicious little twerp was eyeing us like we'd sprouted tentacles. I checked just to make sure... Nope. Good.

"We just need a few things to help us out of our current predicament." I went to a cupboard and started looking for what we needed, not expecting to find it on the first try. Things in galleys—and kitchens, too, for that matter—always seem about as organized as a monorail wreck to me. How do cooks know where to find anything? I knew it would be hard to find the hot mitts, since Mishi didn't use them and he very rarely let anyone else in his galley, but it's kinda hard to hide a twelve-gallon sieve.

"Well, if you'd tell me what you're looking for, I *could* tell you where to look." He put his stubby little fists on his hips and glared. "I *do* know the place pretty well, you know!"

"Well, duh! Sorry, Mish, I should have asked first. We'll be out of here in a second if you just show me where you keep the biggest colander you've got."

"Over there, bottom left." He pointed to a large low cupboard near the huge double sink, and I started to think that maybe cooks weren't as disorganized as I'd thought.

"Oh, yeah, that makes sense!"

I retrieved the colander and hefted it. It was Noodle-O-Rama's® largest model, heavy-gauge stainless and perfect for what I had in mind.

"Thanks, Mish!"

I turned to go, but then stopped upon closer examination of the holey vessel in my hands. A mien of utter shock crossed my features, and I turned to my diminutive culinary employee to express the aforementioned astonishment.

Don't ask *me* why I'm talking like that. Maybe the scotch is too cold.

"This won't do, Mish," I told him, "it's got a crack in it!"

"What?"

You probably know by now what I was planning, so I won't keep you in suspense. The crack was just a lure to get the little fire-hydrant close enough to nab. I knew he was more protective of his galley implements than anything else, so it worked just like I'd hoped. He trundled over, his four little fists flailing, ready to punch out whoever had dented his pot.

"Where? I don't see a—"

I popped it over his head and sat on the top, slick as you please.

"What the *hell* are you doing, Fische!? Let me outta here or I'll have your balls for egg drop soup!"

"Sorry, Mishi, but we need your help for this and I didn't think you'd volunteer." I looked to my stunned comrades. "Get the hot mitts! My ass is starting to scorch!"

"I'll burn you to a (expletive deleted) cinder, you bastard!"

I wasn't joking about the heat. My butt was getting rather warm, so I shifted to standing on the colander. This wasn't easy, since the bottom was round, but I managed not to fall off and free my irate little chef.

"Mishi, we're not going to hurt you, and you'll get a huge bonus for this! Meritorious service under fire, distinguished cooking under adverse conditions, and saving the whole crew under imminent threat of bodily harm. You name it!"

"Name this, you oversized escapee from a B movie! Let me *go*!"

"Get those damn hot mitts over here before my shoes melt!" Kik and Turk were rifling through cupboards and drawers at warp speed, flinging utensils and strange culinary devices in all directions, which undoubtedly enraged Mishi all the more.

Finally they found a store of thick towels, which would just have to suffice; the rubber soles of my shoes were getting a little tacky. Turk pushed down on the top of the colander with a towel and I stepped off, trailing smoke from my sneakers.

"Here!" I said, grabbing a thickly quilted tea-pot cozy from Kik and motioning her to the other side. "Now, tip it up a little, Turk."

You have to understand that this was all done amid a steady stream of Turpenoid profanity, which was making conversation difficult, not to mention making us sweat even more than the galley's torrid temperature.

Turk tilted the colander, and Kik and I grabbed Mishi's legs—well, two of them anyway—and hoisted him up. He promptly reached up and grabbed my wrist, which burned the living crap out of me, but then Turk grabbed two of his arms and we had him relatively immobilized.

"To the airlock! Quick!"

"What the (expletive deleted) are you going to do at the airlock?!" Mishi screamed in a tone high enough to threaten every piece of glass in the galley.

We crashed through the doors and down the corridor, holding the poor screeching Turpenoid splayed out like a sacrificial...uh...Turpenoid, I guess.

"This won't hurt, Mishi!" I yelled, trying to sound reassuring over his torrential screams. "Zook was fine afterward, and you're even going to get a helmet!"

Needless to say, by the time we got to the airlock, we were all pretty badly scorched and Mishi's vocal cords were getting a little raw. He was starting to sound like a kettle that was left to boil after it had already started to toot.

Luckily, when we got there, Zook was standing by with an appropriately sized space-suit helmet already fitted with enough high-temperature duct tape to seal the thing to Mishi's torso. He also had a length of safety line, something I hadn't thought of. Okay, maybe I *am* an evil monster; so fire me.

Oops. Can't... The captain thing, remember?

It took two tries to get the helmet on, since the little hot-pot still had two hands free. Once it was in place and the line attached, it was a simple matter to just throw him out the open airlock.

For a moment I wondered what the hell I was doing. I was about to risk the life of one of my crew without his permission in order to save the rest of us. How could I? Maybe I really was an inhuman monster!

I looked at Mishi's face, screaming obscenities at me from behind the face plate of the helmet; I'd known him for years, and eaten his food for even longer. I would call him as close a friend as I had, and here I was risking all of that. I bit my lip, chided myself for my lack of compassion, and made the right choice.

"One... Two... THREE!"

Mishi vanished into the pulsing nothingness that was stringspace, trailing the safety line behind. It was suddenly very quiet in the airlock.

"Uh, we better hang on. The last time this happened, there was quite a—"

We were suddenly tossed across the airlock like four rag dolls in a bucket, and Mishi's ebony-covered form was flung from the darkness to bounce off the far bulkhead. He lay there squirming on the deck as we struggled to disentangle ourselves.

"Quick, Zook, the emitter!"

Okay, this much I'd actually planned ahead for, believe it or not. Zook and I had discussed the black nothing-stuff that made up inter-string stringspace, and why it wasn't found near strings. The answer had to be gravitons, since that was the only thing strings are made of, and the only other thing in stringspace...I hoped.

Zook grabbed the little gizmo that spewed out gravitons—No, I don't know *why* they make a little gizmo that spews out gravitons, but I knew we had one. They teach you that in captain school—and pointed it at Mishi. I wouldn't have known that he pulled the trigger, except that the black nothing-stuff that coated my cook suddenly oozed off like overheated chocolate frosting and slimed away like an amoeba on cocaine. Zook continued pointing the emitter at the oozy little puddle, chasing it toward the airlock, which seemed as good a place for it as any.

"The blowtorch, Kik!"

She handed it over and I fired it up, playing the tip of the flame lightly over Mishi in an attempt to keep the poor little fella warm.

"Okay, now help him with the helmet, but be careful about the tape; it's gonna hurt coming off."

"Him or us?" Turk said with a curse, burning his fingers before figuring out to use the tongs.

Then, to my utter astonishment, Kik clamped the six-inch coil spanner around the neck of the suit helmet in an attempt to keep the homicidal Turpenoid at bay. In less than a minute, amid much screaming—*most* of it from Mishi—the helmet was off, the airlock's outer door was closed and we were all staring at one another in amusement, satisfaction, fear, rage and, well, who *knew* what Zook thought?

"See?" I said, trying the I-told-you-so ploy. "That wasn't so bad, was it, Mish?"

He glared at me, those four little fists clenching and unclenching as he undoubtedly fantasized about grasping and squeezing various parts of my anatomy. The thought made me want to cross my legs.

"Come on, now, Mishi. You're not hurt, and you're only the second being to ever spacewalk in stringspace! Your name will go down in history!"

He glared some more. I even think I saw steam coming from his little nostrils.

"Think of the bonus! I'll pay you double for the trip, plus all those extras for helping us out of this mess! You'll be rich! You could retire!"

"Or I could sue your ass for every farf you've got, and be even richer!" he growled, cooling down a bit, or maybe heating up, since he seemed to be enjoying the blowtorch.

"Uh, you could, Mish, but I'm kinda broke, remember?"

"Oh, yeah. Laila cleaned you out! Ha! I forgot that you fell for that one!" He turned enough for me to play the flame over his backside. "Maybe I'll just take your ship!"

"Uh, well, it's kinda the company's ship, if you wanna get technical, but they might give it to you as a settlement if you can find a lawyer who'll touch the case." I played the flame up and down, trying my best to placate the little volcano. "We're kind of breaking the law anyway, remember?"

"Double pay, huh?"

"Plus bonuses."

"How much in bonuses?"

"Say, twenty percent of your gross."

"Before or after the doubling?"

"After."

"Fine." He turned away and headed for the inner airlock door, then turned back and glared. "But why the hell chuck *me* out the airlock?"

"You were the only alien onboard besides the Farfnian mud puppies that we keep for testing product." I tried my best trust-me-I'm-your-captain smile, which flopped. "If I'd used the mud puppy, we'd be blinking in on Farfan, which I think you would have enjoyed even less than this."

"What about Charley's pets?"

"Charley has pets?" *Uh-oh*, was all I could think.

"A Corpalian moth beetle, a Druellan web slug, and two Epok zebra darters that he keeps in a tank under his bunk."

I looked at my executive officers and received three unanimous shrugs. Well, crap. How am I supposed to be a good captain if my officers stop being omniscient?

"Uh, sorry about that, Mish. I didn't know."

"Just don't try something like this again, Fische, or I'll serve your brain up for an appetizer."

"Deal." Not like it was doing me any good anyway. "By the way, Mishi. We'll be landing on Turp Prime in a few minutes. Know any good places to eat?"

He looked a little surprised, then realized that I was telling him the truth. "Yeah, a few."

"Then let me buy you dinner."

He looked at me like I'd just grown four extra limbs, then actually smiled—it didn't look like a human smile, but I've known Mishi for a while—and said, "Sure, Harry, but you might have to wear something air-conditioned. It's about three hundred degrees at home this time of year."

"I'll wear my best suit."

He smirked and walked out, and I thought I might have just barely saved our friendship. I hoped so; it'd be a pain to try to find another cook as good as Mishi.

Okay, so maybe I'm a *little* evil.

***

Popping out of stringspace was a little anti-climactic. We were all ready for the worst, strapped in, fired up, locked and loaded, and we blinked in just outside the Turpenoid equivalent of a two-story ranch house with some nice landscaping, a two-car garage, a barn, and a pool. Yeah, the water in it was boiling, and didn't look terribly inviting, but it was a nice touch, and probably was good for property value. I'd brought Mishi up to the bridge, not only to let him see his home world and maybe placate him a bit more, but also to get directions once we re-entered real space.

"Yep, that's home all right!" He played with the viewer, looking around the grounds a bit. It looked like a peaceful enough setting, complete with little Turpenoid vehicles, farm animals, pets, and kid's toys strewn around the yard.

"That's your home, Mishi? I figured we'd pop in next to the local hospital or something."

"Oh, I was laid in a hospital, sure, but Mom and Dad brought me home to be hatched."

"Turpenoids lay eggs?" Hmph, who knew.

"Well, duh!" Mishi just snorted his disgust at my ignorance—I'd been showing it a lot lately, I admit—and looked back at the viewer.

There was a haze of heat rising up off of everything, of course, and the plants and animals were totally alien to me, having evolved in temperatures that would quite literally cook my bacon. But home is where you hang your hat, I always say, and Mishi was obviously pleased with our destination.

"Don't suppose we have time to drop in and see the folks, do we?" he asked, eying me hopefully.

I couldn't very well say 'No', could I?

"I don't think we're in that big a hurry. We've gotta be about a hundred light years ahead of the cheese rustlers. A couple of hours won't hurt. Just let me know where we can put the ship down safely."

"Oh, anywhere's fine. Just don't squash anything."

I relayed the instructions to Kik, and she put us down light as a feather between the barn-looking thing and the garage-looking thing. We fit right in.

"Okay, then, Harry." Mishi ambled toward the lift. "I'll be back in a couple of hours. You can set a course for Teoji, it's the nearest spaceport."

"Great. Say hi to the folks for us!" Before the doors closed, I asked him the only question that was really important. "Oh, and Mish, how close are the crabs watching things around here?"

"Oh, not very. They got what they wanted and kinda leave us alone now." He pushed the button and the doors started to close. "Kind of a shame about all the mountains, though."

"Yeah," I said before the doors closed completely. I looked at the viewer and the virtually flat landscape. Turp Prime hadn't always been that way. It had once had as much topography as any other planet, before the Farfnians found out that there were some very rich mineral deposits under all the mountain ranges.

The Farfnians quickly adopted a strategy to protect the woefully underprotected and vital resources; they would be exported to a safe location. The only problem with getting at them had been the mountains, but that wasn't a problem for the Farfnians.

They leveled the planet.

Oh, it was all done aboveboard, legal and everything. The Turp government earned a tidy sum, most of which is still in the pockets of a few retired Turp politicians, and all the displaced Turpenoids—only a few billion—were given temporary homes...in space.

No wonder Mishi's always in a bad mood. I feel the same way about Earth, and all they did to us was kill off ninety-eight percent of our cows.

"Okay, lady and gents!" I said, breaking the uncomfortable silence and jarring my thoughts out of their depressing spiral— yeah, that could happen. "We need a little brain-storming session regarding our next port of call."

"You want to find the Sploig?" Zook asked, grin in place. The weird little twit.

"Exactly! And not just any old Sploig, I want the ones that stole Tillamook. They could be anywhere in an expanding sphere from Earth, if they use conventional string-based travel, and it'll be next to impossible to find them. It will require significant strategic planning, much forethought, and a good deal of creativity. My bar is at your disposal!"

"All right, I'm in," Kik said, zipping up her last zipper. I hadn't even noticed her getting out of the pilot's couch, that's how preoccupied I was!

CHAPTER FOUR

THE CARPOOLIAN CONNECTION

Six hours and two bottles of Captain Mongo's Spiced Sake™ later, we'd come to one inescapable conclusion: We had to consult the Carpoolians.

Dangerous, no doubt, considering that the surface of Carpool was probably still cooling off from the bombardment that the Farfnians levied right in the middle of our last visit. The Preemptive Punitive Measure—PPM for short; assigning an acronym makes planetary warfare so much more politically correct, don't you think?—decimated the Carpoolian economy, killed millions and put a real kink in the local slime-based ecology. It seems that all the excess heat of several hundred asteroids being dropped on most of the Carpoolian cities had the result of drying out the atmosphere, which killed off about ninety percent of the slime, which, in turn, was the primary production species for the whole planet's ecology.

Don'cha just *hate* it when that happens?

But not to worry! The ever-helpful Farfnians were quick to come to the rescue. Several Farfnian corporations bid on the reconstruction of Carpool. In fact, there are many Farfnian corporations that do nothing *but* rebuild the planetary infrastructures of the planets that their government bombs the living crap out of. Then the corporations return the favor by donating billions of farfs to their benefactor's political campaigns. It's kind of like job security, I think. Anyway, some bid on rebuilding the spaceports, some bid on rebuilding the buildings, and one intrepid company bid on the daunting task of replenishing the planetary supply of slime. There were no counter bids on that job—you think?—so the company could write their own ticket. A several-billion-farf ticket, I might add.

So, as a result of this reconstruction and re-slimation effort, Carpool was virtually crawling with crabs. Not a pretty mental picture, I know.

Now, you might think that this would preempt our trip, but the converse of that was actually the case. The Carpoolians, far from spurning this occupying force, embraced them, welcomed them into their homes and businesses, encouraged them to work and be productive, and, in true Carpoolian fashion, were taking them for every farf they made.

You see, most of the reconstruction crews were just working-class crabs of no particular ambition or connection to their species' galaxy-wide oppression of virtually every other sentient species. And as such, these crabs weren't really our or the Carpoolians' enemies; in fact, they were our *customers*! Not only that, but each and every one of them was displaced from their home world, working way too hard for way too much money, and would undoubtedly feel the immediate need for something to help them forget their miserable existence.

Ahhh, cheese!

So, as you can imagine, when we finally left Turp Prime, we were also ready to deal with the Carpoolians once again.

"Twenty cases of nose plugs?"

"Check," Charley said, marking off the special items I'd purchased.

"Fifty extra gas masks?"

"Check."

"Fifty cans of air freshener?"

"Check."

"Twelve hundred scented pine trees to hang from our rearview mirrors?"

"Uh, check, but..."

"What?" I was impatient. I had captain stuff to do! Stuff like...uh...well, captain stuff!

"We don't have any rearview mirrors, Harry."

"We don't?" I actually *did* know that, but it's irritating when people don't appreciate my humor. It's even more irritating when they don't even realize I'm trying to be funny.

"Uh, no, Harry." Charley was looking at me like I'd slipped a cog, totally oblivious to my attempted hilarity. Who knows, maybe the Turp temp *was* getting to me.

"Well, we can hang them from doorknobs, then."

"Uh, sure, Harry." He was either too dumb to realize that the ship had just as many doorknobs as rearview mirrors, or he was too worried about my sanity to bring it up.

"Take care of the rest of this stuff, would you, Charley? I've got to get to the bridge."

"Sure, Harry!"

He sounded like that was the best news he'd had all day. The lack of adulation that my crew gives me is heartwarming.

I made my way to the bridge, thinking of which route would be best to get from Turp to Carpool. It was only a six-jump trip—we'd have to use regular string-based travel since none of the Turp pet stores I'd visited had any Carpoolian species—but there were more crabs in that stretch of space than in all the oceans of Earth. Yes, that *was* a joke. You can laugh now.

"Kik!" I snapped in a very captain-like manner as I entered the bridge. "Take your clothes off and get to work!"

"About damned time!" She stepped out of her jumper without breaking stride—practice...lots of practice—and slipped into the nest of hair-thin neuro-conducting noodles that lined the pilot's couch.

"Lucky damned noodles," I muttered as I put on my special belt and took my seat. "Everyone else ready?" I plugged myself in and felt the hum of power as the main engines kicked on.

"Ready, Harry!" Turk may lack higher brain functions, but not enthusiasm.

"I suppose," Zook said with a yawn. He sounded bored, which worried me. Zook's dangerous when he's bored. He looks for interesting things to do, and they usually involve things that scare yesterday's breakfast right out of me.

I punched up the link with Teoji traffic control and gave Kik the okay. We were up and out of the atmosphere before you could play a game of pin-the-crime-on-the-liberal, and three minutes later we were in stringspace again, this time firmly attached to a string by our anti-graviton emitter array.

I won't bore you with the details of our trip from Turp to Carpool. There's nothing to do in stringspace except sit and watch the view, which never changes, eat, sleep, and keep yourself from going crazy with any of the myriad entertainment devices we had onboard.

Personally, I play video games. I'm on level two million six in DOOM XXIII, but it's losing its thrill. I hear DOOM XXIV is coming out soon...

The most interesting thing that happened on the way to Carpool was that nothing happened. Every system we blinked through was a potential trap for cheese runners. The Farfnians aren't stupid, really, they just think they're a lot smarter than everyone else, which is stupid. They're not smarter, they just got a head start. They got lucky and crawled out of the slime earlier than the rest of us and now we're paying for it.

But right now I was beginning to think that all of the crabs had gone on vacation.

Then we entered the Carpoolian system and I realized where they'd gone: They were all here.

"Holy (expletive deleted)! There's a (expletive deleted) load of crabs in this (expletive deleted) system!"

I blinked at Turk. Even for him that was a little harsh.

"Uh, could you be a little more specific, Turk? Exactly how many in a (expletive deleted) load?"

"The computer's still counting, but the ships number in the thousands."

"*Thousands?*" I guess my jaw dropped, because when I tried to say something else, all that came out was an unintelligible mixture of vowel sounds and a little drool. I closed my mouth, swallowed, and tried again. "You sure?"

"Well, I'm not sure they're *all* Farfnian ships, but most are." He punched some buttons on his console and nodded. "Yep. Three thousand two hundred forty-one ships in orbit or in transit between the planets. About ninety-five percent show Farfnian signatures."

"That *is* a (expletive deleted) load," I admitted, leaning back in my seat and considering our options. I was still considering when the comm system bleeped for attention and made up my mind for me.

"Vessel closing on an intercept course, Harry," Turk informed me, poking buttons. "It's an in-system patrol ship. Small."

"Welcoming committee?" I asked, looking at the blinking light on the console as if I could tell whether the crab on the line was a good crab or a bad crab. Or a bad crab who would be willing to be good. Or a good crab who could be... Well, you get the picture.

"What do you want me to do, Harry?" That was Kik. She could see the approaching ship through her much more limited sensors and wanted to know if we were going to make a run for it.

"Just hold course and speed, Kik. We'll play along for now." I keyed the channel open and put on my happy face. "This is Captain Fische, SVIC *Limburger*. Can I help you today?"

"Transmit your IPCC license and manifest, immediately."

"Of course! I'll see right to it!" I had neither, but I was confident that Zook could whip up a reasonable forgery in a heartbeat. Sometimes it is nice having him aboard, when he's not trying to get us killed for fun.

I knew this crab would be no trouble. After so many years of this game, you know when you're looking at a crab who can be bought. This poor chitin-covered cretin wasn't even an officer in the Farfnian Space Navy. He was a petty officer in the Planetary Police Force. "Will you be inspecting our cargo today?"

"What is your cargo?"

"Entertainment equipment." That was close enough to pass the lie detection equipment that was undoubtedly recording and analyzing every word I said.

"For the Carpoolians? What do Carpoolians use for entertainment?"

"Oh, no. Not for the Carpoolians, my good Farfnian. This is specially designed entertainment for your own noble species!

We've heard how hard all the cr—uh, Farfnians are working to restore the Carpoolian worlds, so we thought they could use a little entertainment to make the work pass much more enjoyably."

"What *kind* of entertainment?"

"The *best* kind, my good Farfnian."

We eyed one another for a few dozen heartbeats—mine, not his—and I saw a tiny bit of drool escape his mandibles.

I had him.

"I will personally inspect this entertainment equipment," he said with a perfectly straight face. "Please prepare to dock with my vessel."

"My pleasure, Captain. Our docking port is on the starboard side. We'll be ready in five minutes."

"Very well." He broke the connection.

"He said 'please'," Turk said, blatantly awed. "Crabs never say 'please'."

"This one did." I grinned and punched the key to the intercom. "Charley, break out a couple of bricks of Velveeta®, we're having some company." I closed the link and stood.

"Kik, please zero our thrust and prepare a standard docking maneuver." She made a noncommittal sound of assent in my head through her connection with the pilot's interface.

Yes, I *could* have said, "She said, Uh-huh," but what's the fun in that?

"Need company, Harry?" Turk asked, grabbing a gun from the locker and looking altogether too enthusiastic for my taste.

"No, I've got another job for you, Turk." He looked crestfallen, but nodded. Good boy...here's a biscuit. "Open a secure channel to Neezl and see if his office is still standing. I'd like to talk with him about finding our wayward Tillamook."

"Sure, Harry."

Zook was down in the engineering spaces fiddling with something, so he couldn't ask to come with me, which was also good. Zook tends to piss off authority figures just for the entertainment value, which isn't what I would call healthy.

Sometimes I get nervous when things run so smoothly. This wasn't one of those times. I should have known better.

***

Bribing the Farfnian was child's play. He took his two bricks of processed cheese-food and actually thanked me. Such a nice crab.

He left me his card, just in case I was planning a future trip.

It's good to make new friends, don't you think?

We were undocked—un-docked? de-docked?? Hmmm. Well, the two ships were separated and my new friends were on their way before I even got back to the bridge. Kik had taken the initiative to resume our former course, a lazy-loop orbital approach to the Carpoolian home world.

Turk looked a little frazzled. I figured it was either trying to decipher the communications board or tying his shoes that had done it, but I turned out to be wrong.

"What's up, Turk?"

"Uh, well, I got hold of Neezl."

"Good!"

"He's changed professions."

"Bad!"

"He's running for president."

"Of the planet?"

"Uh, the whole system, I think." Turk scratched his head; maybe his was starting to get warm, too. I know my brain was generating some heat. "Seems the Farfnians gave the Carpoolians the same deal they gave us: form a single government or die. So they're having an election."

"The *Carpoolians* are having an *election*?"

Let me qualify the sheer amount of "Holy crap!" in that statement: Carpoolians don't like governments. They've never had a government, and have certainly never had an election. It's not good for business. Governments charge taxes in order to operate, which infringes on profits, which is the Carpoolian equivalent of scraping fingernails on an old-fashioned chalk board. The closest they've ever come to a governmental institution is a board of directors, but even those don't tend to last very long. Too much bureaucracy.

"Uh, yeah. It's caused quite a stir."

"I can imagine!" No I couldn't, but I was about to find out. "And Neezl's a candidate? Well, if he wins, it could be very good for us. I've never had a president for a business associate before." To think that gaining the presidency would curtail Neezl's illicit dealings in cheese, stolen merchandise, and information would be ridiculous. Gaining public office doesn't even stop *humans* from doing those things.

"Yeah, but there are a lot of candidates."

"Oh? Is it still the primaries?"

"Oh, no. The general election is on for a month from now, but he's still got a lot of competition."

"How much?"

"Well, there are four hundred fifty-two candidates. That's three hundred ninety-seven political parties and a few independents." He scratched his head again. "It's a little confusing, even without looking at the issues."

"I can imagine." There I go again, thinking I have an imagination. Foolish me. "So, is he worried that we'll tarnish his political reputation and telling us to bugger off?"

"Uh, no. He invited us to his campaign headquarters for dinner."

"Uh-oh!"

"What?"

"He's hedging for a campaign contribution."

"Oh, well, yeah. I kinda figured that, Harry. But you could say what you just gave that patrol-boat captain was a 'contribution'. A bribe's a bribe, no matter what you call it."

"I prefer to think of it as an investment." I sat and tried to think of all the angles this could present. We had a hold full of the most valuable commodity in the galaxy, maybe even enough to buy a presidential election. Hmmmm... The possibilities were mind boggling.

"Uh, Harry?"

44

"Yes, Turk." He was starting to bug me. I mean, I was thinking! Rare event, so don't laugh.

"We're not here for business; we're here to find Tillamook."

"Oh, yeah. Yeah, we will. But one doesn't often get the opportunity to shape a government."

"You mean *buy* a government?"

"Same thing."

Did I mention that I'm a greedy bastard? No? Well, I am. Not evil, but greedy. I never bought the idea that greed was one of the seven deadly sins. And sloth? I can't get behind that one, either. And whoever put lust on the list was definitely a prude. And envy? Oh, come on! Envy's just wanting something better than what you've got! And when you get it, what's wrong with being proud about it? And while we're at it, gluttony? Just because I eat more than I need to eat, I'm evil? This whole thing makes me angry! Oops, there's the seventh one. And did you notice how little things like bigotry, puppy-kicking, and breaking someone's heart who loved you didn't make the cut? I mean, come on! Who compiled this list anyway?

Huh? Oh, yeah, back to the story. Sorry, I got going there, didn't I?

"So, where is Neezl's campaign headquarters? Should we dress for the occasion?" I kicked my feet up (sloth), opened a bag of Chee-Toes® (gluttony), didn't offer Turk any (greed), had some impure thoughts about my pilot (lust), thought about Riffy, her last beau (envy), which reminded me of Laila (angry), but I'm over that and moving on (pride). Wheew! That was exhausting!

"Well, I don't think going *naked* would be a good idea." The sad part is he wasn't joking. "And it's in the same place his old headquarters were."

"Oh, cripes. You're kidding me?"

"Nope. He still works out of The Inferno."

"Great. Well, I guess that answers the question about what to wear. Full weapons and body armor, Turk. And pick out something nice for me." I plugged in and told Kik where to land as my security officer chortled with glee. Yes, I'm sure it was a chortle, and I'm considering putting that on my list of sins. Thou shalt not chortle. Yes, I like the sound of that.

Kik was almost as gleeful as Turk, which wasn't astonishing. Any time we go out, she gets positively atwitter. "You want me to dress for success, I suppose." Sure, she *sounded* surly about it, but there was plenty of twitter underneath.

"That would be nice, Kik, but don't go overboard, please." Actually, it's quite an advantage having Kik along on a jaunt like this. Everyone looks at her, not me. In fact, it's hard to get anyone's attention when Kik's *dressed*, no matter what I'm wearing. It's kind of like striking a match in a burning house; it goes unnoticed.

I just hope she never finds out that I use her for very attractive camouflage. My nose still hurts.

***

Kik managed to land the ship without rupturing any of my internal organs. The prospect of going out must have put her in a good mood.

"Okay, people, let's get ready!"

"I'll go get dressed," Kik said, hopping out of the pilot's couch, grabbing her jumper, and padding off to the lift. I hoped she planned to put it on in the lift. I'd hate to have to treat any of my male crew members for cardiac arrest.

"Here you go, Harry." Turk handed me the same heavy rifle thingy I'd used when we rescued Kik, but I really didn't feel like lugging the thing around.

"Uh, I was thinking of something a little smaller, actually. Maybe pistol-sized?"

"Oh. Sure." He took the rifle back and stashed it in the weapons locker, turning back to me with a thing that looked like a small satellite dish strapped to a fusion-powered Vegimatic™. There were more buttons and dials on it than on the whole communications console.

"Uh, something a little less complex?" What I knew about guns consisted of, 'This is the dangerous end.'

"Okay. Hmmm." He scratched his chin and picked out a slim little thing that had a trigger on one end and a pointy thing on the other end.

"What is it?" I looked at the tip, which I assumed was the dangerous end. There was a hole in it just about the size of a period. Yeah, like that one.

"A needler. It shoots little slivers of metal. Lots of them."

"Poisonous?"

"Well, duh! It wouldn't do much damage otherwise!" Turk was getting a little frustrated, which is never good.

"Uh, I don't really feel like poisoning anyone, Turk. Don't you have any regular 'gun' guns?"

"What, you mean like old-fashioned use-a-burning-chemical-to-throw-a-hunk-of-lead-at-barely-supersonic-speed guns?"

"Uh, yeah. That's what I was thinking."

He looked back at his arsenal and frowned. I didn't want him to burst a blood vessel, so I made a compromise.

"Tell you what, Turk, I'll stick to these." I picked up my emergency-zero-gee belt with its two cans of Jiffy-Whip® and strapped it on.

"Whipped topping? You're going to walk into The Inferno wearing whipped topping as your only weapon?"

"I hadn't planned on shooting anyone, Turk. If it comes down to it, that's your job." I patted his huge armored shoulder, hoping I hadn't insulted him. "Besides, weapons are mostly for show, and nobody's going to know what these are." I patted the little cylindrical cans at my hips. They were slung low for an easy quick-draw, and only the little red plastic caps showed. Yeah, they *could* be weapons!

"I will." He reached for his linguini blaster and his helmet.

"Well, with your helmet on, nobody's going to know how embarrassed you are, okay?"

"Fine." He put his helmet on and sealed it. "Who else is coming?"

"Oh, just the three of us, I think." We boarded the lift and headed for the airlock. We'd have to take a cab to the club, but it was only a few blocks. "I told Zook to stay here and watch the ship."

"Good." Turk didn't like Zook's risk-taking either, it seemed. That was good by me. In situations like this, having an Immortal along could be deadly, as odd as that sounds.

We exited the lift and found Kik waiting there for us.

I was impressed.

Not so much with her outfit, which *did* leave me gaping like a freshly landed flounder, but with the fact that she'd been able to put it on in less than twelve hours. You see, the most substantial portion of the whole thing was the boots. In fact, the *whole* outfit was the boots. They were black platforms with thick treaded soles, and the tops were straps with fringe. The straps kept going up, winding around and around in strategic crisscross patterns, all the way up to her neck and down her arms. The fringe varied in length and density, exposing a lot, but hiding everything that was important to remain hidden. When she moved, I got little glimpses of those hidden areas. I can't imagine that it was comfortable, but it was definitely Kik.

Oh, and there was jewelry, too. Lots of it. And she wore two standard laser pistols tucked through the straps somewhere, I think. I can't really remember.

"Nice outfit," I said, trying not to stare. You know, I see her *sans* clothing every time she gets into or out of the pilot's couch, and while that is certainly alluring, there is something to be said for a truly stunning woman in an incredibly sensuous outfit.

I love my job.

"Thanks." She handed me a gas mask and put hers on. It didn't help the outfit, but the Carpoolian atmosphere would have us heaving in no time, so it was a necessary accessory.

The cab ride to The Inferno was uneventful, if somewhat horrifying. I don't want to give you the visual image of the horrors that lurk in the back seat of a Carpoolian cab, but we managed to get in, ride four blocks, and get out without touching anything overtly nasty. Kik actually hovered in the air through the whole ride, I swear. Me, I didn't worry. I'd have to burn this jumper anyway.

One thing that did surprise me on the drive was the amount of political advertising plastered on every building, road, sign, and flying object; our cab displayed three different adverts. Even the buildings that were still crumbling from the Farfnian assault had slogans painted on them. The candidates were pulling no punches with their campaigns either. Many were blatantly slanderous, nasty, accusative, and repugnant. Some were even true! I know, hard to believe.

We walked into The Inferno and I knew instantly that we were in over our heads.

I mean, you can tell a place is rough if the clientele are rough-looking and the staff is armed. You can tell a place is *really* rough if the clientele are armed and the staff is behind six inches of Armor-Glass®. You can tell a place is just *way* too rough if the band is armed. Throw into the mix that this was campaign headquarters for a system-wide presidential bid, complete with banners, slogans, guards, and a voter registration booth—with revolving door, of course—and I truly thought that the place had finally earned its name.

And I didn't particularly care for the music, either.

Although the guitarist *was* human and wearing an interesting outfit that consisted mostly of tattoos and clips of ammunition. She gave a whole new meaning to the term "dressed to kill". The music was something they call screech-and-roll. If you remember Earth before the Farfnians landed, it was kind of like a heavy metal polka on methamphetamine.

Kik fit right in.

Amazing that neo-goth became so popular with the alien lowlife crowd.

For once, I was glad to have Turk at my side. At least next to him, my outfit looked swank.

Another surprise was that about a third of the clientele were Farfnians. Only a few weren't wearing standard work clothes, and those wore some kind of slap-together security guard-type uniform. I imagine most of the corporations had their own security. I wondered whose these were, but not very much. As long as they were paid for we'd be fine, and everything in Neezl's domain was paid for. I risked taking off my gas mask since the few humans in the place weren't wearing them. The air was a little thick, but not really nauseating.

"Captain Fisssssche!"

Neezl rounded a table and oozed over, tentacles extended for the ritual embrace. Another jumper bites the dust. It slimed me with much enthusiasm. Eeew.

"Congratulations on your nomination, Neezl!" I said while trying to disentangle myself from its ropy sliminess. "How did you manage it?"

"Well, I've got *you* to thank for that, my good human."

"Me?" I couldn't help but smile. Humble really isn't me.

"Yesss you, Harry!" It guided us toward a large table near the back corner. "The…uh…product you sssold me on your lassst trip out tripled in value the inssstant the crabsss bombed usss." It waved a tentacle at the over-decorated room. "That transssaction has financed thisss entire campaign! I'm ssso far ahead of the competition that they can't even sssmell me anymore!"

Carpoolian humor. I'll never get it.

Kik and Turk accompanied us, but Kik's eyes were on the dance floor—be still my pounding heart…okay, maybe it wasn't my heart that was pounding—and Turk was scanning the crowd like he was looking for someone to shoot. Well, I suppose he was. It *was* his job, after all. And Turk took his job very seriously.

We sat down.

Well, Kik and I sat down. Turk took up station with his back in the corner, his visor sweeping the crowd slowly from left to right and back. I'm glad he was happy. It made me feel a little more secure to know that his were probably the only eyes in the place that were watching something besides my pilot. That included Neezl's guards, the band, and the waitstaff. I was as good as invisible.

There was one thing, however, that I was not prepared for, and that was the food. Sitting down to dinner with a Carpoolian has to be one of the best appetite suppressants in the galaxy. It wasn't the food. The wait staff put plates of entirely Earth-like delicacies in front of us that looked very yummy. The food they put in front of

Neezl, however, was more to Carpoolian tastes, and watching it eat ten pounds of rotten sea slugs in port wine sauce was enough to make me want to have my mouth sewn shut.

But we had to suffer through it. Dinner is the only thing that will induce a Carpoolian to put business on the back burner, and there was a strict etiquette of "eat first, deal second" that had to be followed. I sat and pushed things around my plate, sipping water and trying not to barf. Kik actually nibbled. Well, I guess her stomach is stronger than mine. Must be the company she keeps.

When dinner was done we were offered genuine Earth-grown, hand-made cigars. I accepted one gratefully, as did Kik, not because either of us really wanted to smoke, but because cigar smoke is one of the most pungent smells I know, and after only one puff, I couldn't smell anything but my stogie.

Ahhh, olfactory bliss...

"Ssso, Harry!" Neezl began, picking its rows of teeth with a tentacle. "I can't sssay that I exsssspected you to return sssso ssssoon."

"Something's come up," I said in that semi-conspiratorial tone that said, 'Something's come up.'

Uh...yeah.

"What isss thisss thing that hasss come up that isss ssso important to bring you all the way to Carpool?" It eyed us with enough scrutiny to make me uncomfortable. "Sssurely it wasssn't this little political nonssssenssse that we have been forced into."

"No, Neezl. To tell you the truth, I didn't even know Carpool was having an election." I puffed my stogie and blew a perfect smoke ring. "This is something else entirely."

"I'm all earsss!"

Actually, it was much more tentacles than ears, but I knew what it meant.

"You remember Tillamook?"

"Your competition, if I remember correctly."

"Until about a week ago. It's gone."

"The crabsss found them out, huh?" It waved its squidy mouth parts in a gesture that I knew signified remorse.

51

"Well, we don't really think so. At least Zook, my engineer, doesn't think so. He thinks Tillamook was stolen."

I could have dropped a half ton of rotten oysters in Neezl's lap and it wouldn't have noticed. I'd hit a nerve.

"Sss...ssstolen? Sssurely you jessst, Harry! How could one sssteal an entire production facility?"

"Beats the hell out of me, but we're going to find out and bring the whole thing back home." I pretended to ignore his writhing mouthparts, a sure sign of nervousness. "That's why we came to you, Neezl, my friend. We need your help."

"Help is exsssspensssive, Harry. And I wouldn't know where to ssstart looking."

"We have some theories, and I'm sure that you have the connections. It'd be a pretty hard item to move on the black market, but we think the thieves might have taken it for personal reasons."

"Persssonal reasssonsss?" It did the Carpoolian equivalent of a shrug. "I'm not sssure what you mean, Harry."

I was quite sure it knew exactly what I meant at that point. Carpoolian body language is very expressive, and something that they take pride in reading in one another. What most Carpoolians don't realize is that we can learn to read it, too. Neezl was giving off every sign of being both nervous and evasive. It was my job to make the nervousness go away, and make him want to be forthcoming about what he knew, which, I was betting, was plenty. And there's only one way to make a Carpoolian do anything.

"How is the campaign going, by the way?" I looked around at the highly decorated room.

"I have dissscovered that politicsss is exsssspenssssive, Harry. I'm putting every farf I have into thisss, and ssstill, my competition isss ssssliming down my neck."

"And what are the rules about campaign contributions?"

"Rulesss?" It did the shrug thing again. "How can there be rulesss when there isss money involved?"

Good point.

"Then I will cease to beat around the bush," I said, leaning across the table and shifting my voice into that conspiratorial tone that told everyone who was watching us that the deal was going down.

"And why would you pummel a ssshrub?" Neezl asked, blowing my suave composure right out the door.

"It's a figure of speech, Neezl. It means that I will try to start being more direct."

"Pleassse do, Harry."

"I'm carrying the same load I was the last time I visited Carpool." I paused dramatically.

"Yesss? And..."

"And I will donate half of it to your campaign coffers if you find whoever stole Tillamook." Considering the inflated price of cheese, I thought that a very generous offer.

"Three quartersss."

Now the gloves were off; we were past the introductions and into the haggling phase. I could barely suppress a grin.

"Two thirds."

"Thirteen eighteenthsss."

"Eleven sixteenths." Ha...try to fool *my* cybernetic brain, will you!

"Twenty-five thirty-fifthssss."

"Forty-nine seventy-firsts." Touché

"Fifty-nine eighty-fourthsss! And that'sss my final offer! Unlessss you want to throw in the ssservicesss of your pilot again."

"I don't care if you've got a whole Shesharrian delegation that needs entertaining, Neezl. Kik's not on the bargaining block this time." I felt my pilot's fingernails on my forearm, but I kept my eyes on Neezl.

"Uh, Harry?"

"Not this time, Kik!"

"Uh, it's not that. I think we've got trouble."

Neezl and I broke eye contact simultaneously. We both looked toward the entrance to the club where two very large figures were descending the shallow steps onto the main floor. They were positively huge—Turk-sized and then some—tripedal and six-armed. And they were wearing the strangest body armor I'd ever seen. It scintillated through a rainbow of colors right before our eyes; hard to look at without getting dizzy.

"Oh, crap! They've found me!"

That was Neezl, and if anything could take my attention from our new visitors, it was the tone of the Carpoolian's voice. It was about to lose its rotten sea slugs, if I was any gauge of Carpoolian sphincter control.

"You *know* them?"

"Uh, yesss, Harry. And I'm sssorry to sssay that they were the lassst people I encountered who were inquiring about Tillamook."

Now I was worried about my own sphincter control.

"Uh, and just when was it that they were asking about Tillamook?"

"About three weeksss ago."

"And do you have any idea who they are?"

"Yes, Harry, they are the— Uh-oh! They've spotted me!" It got up from the table.

"The who, Neezl?" I said, grabbing one of his tentacles.

"You wouldn't believe me if I told you, Harry." It pulled away and started to ooze toward the bar.

"They're the Sploig, aren't they?"

It stopped in its slimy little tracks.

"How did you know?"

"Just a guess." I stood with the intention of discretely following my Carpoolian friend to his secret exit. No, I didn't *know* where his secret exit was. It was *secret*! I just knew that if this was my place, I'd certainly have one, and that's where I'd be going right now. My companions moved with me, knowing that we were suddenly in very deep trouble.

That was when one of the Sploig pointed a finger at us, something went sizzle and Neezl exploded.

Kik screamed.

Turk fired.

And all I could think was that this would really put a dent in Neezl's run for president.

CHAPTER FIVE

OUT OF THE FRYING PAN

In the span of only a few heartbeats I was astounded on three counts: First, I was amazed that everyone in the place but me seemed to be firing some kind of weapon all at the same time. Second, it looked like the Sploig were completely unaffected by the barrage of bullets, energy, and bad language. Third, I had discovered that Carpoolians smell even worse on the inside than the outside.

Eeeewwwww.

I wiped bits of sizzling slime from my face and stared in astonishment. There was nothing left of Neezl but a few bits of fried tentacle. He'd been obliterated.

There went my shot at influencing the future Carpoolian government.

Well, at least the music had stopped.

I was trying to see the bright side.

The *reason* the music had stopped was because every member of the band had traded his or her instrument for one or two firearms, and were blazing away at the Sploig. They must have gotten their attention, because the Sploig behind the one who'd blasted Neezl into fried calamari raised one arm and gestured at the quartet. The air sizzled and the accordionist exploded in a screeching E-flat, the drummer caught some shrapnel from the explosion and went down, the bass player dropped his gun and ran, and the guitarist dove for cover, twin machine pistols chattering, her guitar still slung over her shoulder. The bullets were having all the effect of bugs on a windshield.

Then something hit me.

55

No, I mean something *really* hit me, and hard!

I found myself lying behind the bar with something warm and pleasantly lumpy atop me. Kik rolled off—drat!—pistols blazing lavender fire, fringe flying as she swore a blue streak.

What a woman.

"What the hell're ya doin', Harry?" she yelled, moving and firing as a large portion of the bar vanished in sizzling splinters.

"Nothing!" I dusted myself off and tried to sit up, but she knocked me down with one of her boots. "Ow! What was that for?"

"Well, if you're not going to do anything, stay the hell down!"

Not a half-bad suggestion.

I rolled and squirmed around the corner of the bar, peeking around it to take in the mayhem. Most of the club's occupants were either down, dead, fled, or firing at the two seemingly invulnerable Sploig. Turk, I noticed, was doing an admirable job with his linguini blaster as he dodged and rolled and fired repeatedly. He really was very good. Every time one of the Sploig gestured at him, he dove out of the way.

The walls were taking a beating, though.

The muzzle of Turk's weapon was glowing blue-white. He had the thing dialed up to the highest setting, and every time he fired, the club was bathed in light. The bolts from the thing were enough to punch through a ship's hull, and they seemed to be having some effect on the two aliens. Their armor had stopped shifting in color, and started to glow a dull red. They were heating up.

I squirmed quickly back around the bar, behind Kik—okay, I *did* linger there for a moment, but just to admire the view—and around the other end. There were quite a few more patrons hiding back here, but I wasn't looking for conversation; I was looking for the damn exit! Neezl had been heading this way before he'd been sizzled, and I knew he wasn't coming back here to mix drinks.

"Hey! Watch it!"

"Oh, sorry." I'd bumped into someone. Real estate back here was at a premium, and every time the Sploig sizzled, a piece of the bar went away, making it that much more dear. The person I'd bumped into was squatting amid a pile of empty ammunition clips, and her outfit was greatly diminished. "Hey, you're the guitarist!"

"And you're a freaking genius!" She adjusted the hang of her instrument, dumped two clips, jacked in two new ones, and popped up to empty them at the Sploig. "Who're you? And why aren't you firing?"

"I'm Harry, and I'm not firing because I'm only armed with these." I indicated my holster.

"Grenades?" Two more clips hit the floor, and two more were taken from her outfit. I tried not to stare at the interesting mixture of leather and tattoo that was revealed.

"Jiffy Whip™," I said, pulling out a can. I popped the nozzle and squirted a bit into my mouth. "I'm hypoglycemic."

"Well, I'm agnostic. Nice to meet you." She popped up and emptied two more clips. "So what the hell are you doing back here?"

"Looking for an exit."

"Good luck!" She reloaded. The pictures on her skin were being revealed bit by bit every time she did this, and it was kind of like one of those video puzzles that reveals a bit of a map or painting with every riddle you answer. Nice effect. "So why do you *really* carry around cans of whipped topping?"

"Emergency zero-gee maneuvering." She looked at me like I'd said something funny. See what I get for being serious? "No. Really. The gravity on my ship tends to go out occasionally. Just squirt the opposite direction you want to float."

"Kind of messy, isn't it?" She popped up and fired again, and a piece of the wall behind her vanished into slag. The Sploig had taken notice.

"Not as messy as getting vaporized. What do you think you're accomplishing with those anyway?" I indicated her smoking firearms with a nod. "I mean, I might as well use this!" I hefted a can, miming to throw it at the marauding aliens.

"Well, I'm spoiling their aim some, anyway. Keeps them off the big guy with the Farfnian blaster. He's the only one in here doing any good!" She popped up, but didn't fire, then looked down at me with 'I just had an idea' written plainly on her face.

"Throw it!"

"Huh?" Okay, I was regressing. All the weapons fire was making me goofy.

"Throw the can, Harry!"

I looked at the can of Jiffy Whip™ in my hand, then back at her. "Where?"

"Where do you (expletive deleted) think?"

I glanced through a hole in the bar at the two raging Sploig; their armor was glowing cherry red now. I looked at the can in my hand and realized what she was thinking. I crouched, took careful aim and threw.

I have to credit her marksmanship—markswomanship?—it's hard to hit a flying object with a machine pistol, or at least that's what they tell me. She sprayed the can with hollow-point rounds, and it exploded right before it hit the alien's armor. Sugar and synthetic-milk byproducts sprayed the glowing hot armor, caramelizing into a black crusty mess on impact. Arms flailed wildly, sizzling randomly. The Sploig was blinded.

"Nice shot!" That was Kik, grinning like a punk rock girl with a new whip.

"Again!" the guitarist yelled, ejecting two empty clips and slamming two more into place. More tattoo was revealed, and I was starting to get a better view of the 'big picture' before she said, "Throw it!"

I flicked the little red cap off my last can of Jiffy Whip™, took careful aim, and let fly. While the blinded alien flailed around...well...blindly, the other was still busily attempting to sizzle my security officer, so it never saw the sugary missile coming. Unfortunately that also meant that it was facing slightly away from us. When the can went off under the uncanny aim of my newly acquainted musical markswoman, it spattered only half of the beastie's "head".

"Crap!" she screamed as the thing turned all three of its sizzlers on us in retribution.

I couldn't have said it better.

I pushed Kik one way while I lunged the other, just as a large section of the bar disintegrated into splinters and dust. Guitar Lady and I rolled to rest only mildly—and rather pleasantly—entangled in one another. It was short-lived, however, for the Sploig was quickly chewing away at the bar with two of its sizzlers while the other fired wildly at Turk, who was running out of things to hide behind.

"Got any more whipped topping?"

"I'm fresh out!" Then I remembered the lunch I hadn't touched, and realized that the club was also a restaurant. "Where's the kitchen?"

Her eyes lit up like it was Christmas and I was Santa Claus. I have that effect on women a lot. Uh-huh. Then she astonished me by slamming her steel-toed boot into the back of the bar, smashing the thin cabinetry into splinters. As if the Sploig weren't doing enough damage to the place.

"Here!" she shouted gleefully, dragging out a canister that was labeled "Danger! Contents Under Pressure. Do Not Incinerate. May Cause Tooth Decay."

"Throw this!"

I hefted the canister, then looked at the distance to the Sploig. Who did she think I was? Turk? The thing must have weighed twenty kilos.

"How 'bout I roll it?"

"How 'bout I help it along?" She jacked in two more clips and nodded, grinning. Yep, they were nice tattoos all right. First-rate work. Real art!

"Ah-hem!"

Oops. Busted.

"Sorry, I've just never seen ink-work like that." Yeah, good excuse.

"Just roll the can, Cheese Boy. You can gawk at my ink later."

"Deal!" I hefted the heavy cylinder, lunged up over the remnants of the bar and heaved it in the general direction of the Sploig.

I ducked just as something sizzled over my head and Guitar Lady dove around the corner of the bar and opened up. Bullets riddled the rolling canister, speeding it on its way and sending high-fructose corn syrup and caramel coloring spraying in every direction. The sticky syrup doused the flailing aliens, coating them in caramelized sugar.

And the crowd went wild!

Actually, the Sploig were only slightly less dangerous, spraying the room with fire just to keep everyone at bay. It worked for me. I ducked and stayed ducked. But several others were taking the opportunity to bring their weapons to bear, taking aim and firing careful bursts at the joints of the glowing, caramelized armor.

I watched as Turk stepped from behind a concrete pillar, adjusted the noodles of his weapon and took careful aim. He fired a pencil-thin beam of energy so bright that I had to shut my eyes. When I opened them, one of the aliens was minus a leg. There was no blood, and the thing stayed standing, albeit wobbling slightly, but Turk was taking aim again.

The aliens had had enough.

They turned to one another and gestured with their arms. An energy field flickered into existence around them, but only for an instant. Then there was nothing there at all. No Sploig, no bodies, no blood... Just one very ruined club and a lot of dead and shot-up patrons. Not to mention the proprietor.

"Damn!"

I looked at Guitar Lady, the question plain on my face.

"They got away!"

"Uh, I think *we* got away," I said, dusting off my ruined jumper and standing. I offered her a hand. "What's your name anyway?"

She put her guns away, took the hand and stood, dusting off the remnants of her outfit. There really was a lot more to it than just web gear and ammo. I mean, there was more than there was to Kik's outfit.

"Call me Kely. Thanks." I hadn't noticed it because we'd both been hugging the floor like a long-lost relative, but she was a good bit taller than me. Not that I'm intimidated by taller women or anything, it's just that...well, okay, so I'm a *little* intimidated when I've got to look up to avoid staring a woman right in the chest. She was a lot taller than me. "I've got to see about my band."

"Sure."

She smiled and waded through the destruction to the podium where her band had been. There wasn't a lot left, just a few shards of accordionist and a drummer riddled with black and white keys; the detonating accordion had really done some damage. The bass player had done what bass players do when the fertilizer hits the air conditioning; he'd hit the road.

"We should go." Kik holstered her pistols and gave a little total-body shiver that straightened all of her fringe in one simple motion, and was *way* too sexy to describe with mere words.

No, I am *not* drooling! I spilled my drink!

"Uh, yeah." I focused my eyes on something besides fringe-clad flesh and said, "And thanks for the, uh...tackle thing. You probably saved my life."

"No probably about it, Harry." She gave me The Look, which made me feel ever-so-much better. "I mean, what were you thinking? You were standing there like a deer in the headlights!"

"Hey, don't forget whose zero-gee-acceleration packs saved the day here!" I patted my empty holsters. "If I hadn't been packing whipped topping, we'd all be sizzled."

"Fair enough." She scanned the demolished club. At least she was giving it The Look and not me. "I don't suppose you've got a comm link. We should have Zook send a car."

"Good idea, but I don't know about sitting here waiting for it." I nodded to the vast majority of the club's remaining clientele, who were wasting no time in departing the premises. "This place is going to be crawling with crabs in no time."

"Would you look at this!" Turk exclaimed, stepping into our conversation with all the delicacy of a bull moose in a Pottery Barn®. He thrust a piece of glowing hot metal at me, very nearly burning my eyebrows off. It looked like a chrome-plated lamp base with three little prongs for feet. The top end was fried, however, and wires and other mechanical and electronic insides were sizzling and popping.

"Nice." I backed to a safe distance. "What is it?"

"It's the piece of one of those (expletive deleted) Sploig that I shot off! Look!" He thrust the smoldering end at me again. This was starting to become not only dangerous, but annoying as well. Kind of like Turk.

"Yes, Turk. I see. It's very nice. Maybe you can mount it on a plaque on your wall aboard the *Limburger*, assuming we get back to the ship in one piece. Now, could you patch a call through to—"

"No! Damn it, Harry!" He popped the seals on his helmet and wrenched it off his head. I guess he felt the need to glare at me eye-to-eye, which he did quite vehemently. "Look at the burnt end. See any blood? Any bone or cooked meat?"

I looked.

Sometimes I'm such an idiot.

"Holy crap!" I reached out and almost took the hot piece of metal in my bare hands, then realized that third-degree burns probably wouldn't make the situation better.

"Yeah. Holy crap."

"You mean they were (expletive deleted) robots?" Kik had joined the Holy Crap Club.

"Looks that way." I took a little closer look, poking at a few sputtering wires with a stylus from my pocket. It was all mechanical and electronics, sure enough. "We've got to get this to Zook. He'll have some idea what the hell those things were."

"Who's Zook, and what the hell's that?" Guitar Lady was back, and she'd made our threesome a foursome with about the same aplomb as I had come to expect from my security officer. "By the way, nice shootin', big guy." She slapped Turk on the back with enough force to actually move him an inch or so. I was impressed.

"Thanks. You too." Evidently so was Turk; his attention snapped from the mysterious Sploig/robot leg in his hand to Kely in the span of a heartbeat. "Great idea with the compressed soda canister."

"Thanks. I'm Kely."

"Turk."

"Nice to meet you, Turk."

"Same here." They shook hands. I think if I'd have had the presence of mind to slip a lump of coal in between their palms, I'd have had a diamond.

Ain't butch love cute?

"I hate to break this up, but we really should get back to our ship, Kely. We're not exactly here on legitimate business, and when the crabs get here..."

"Oh, yeah, I don't suppose cheese runners are popular with the Farfnians, especially with all the election stuff going on."

"Who said we were cheese runners?" Then I remembered our conversation during the firefight. "And you called me Cheese Boy earlier! How did you know?"

"Oh, come on!" She poked a thumb at Turk, then another at Kik. "Full armored security complete with Farfnian weaponry and a pilot dressed to distract, all coming in here to meet with Neezl the Weasel. Did you think everyone would just assume you were selling magazine subscriptions?"

"Okay, so we're not subtle. But, in point of fact, you're wrong. We aren't running cheese. Not on this trip."

"What then?"

"Well, actually—"

"No time, Harry. We gotta go." Kik grabbed my arm, all fingernails, which is enough to get anyone's attention. Then I heard it, too. The piercing four-note bleat of Farfnian security sirens, and they were getting louder.

"Sorry, Kely, but we're late for not getting arrested." I gave Turk The Look—yes, I can do it, too—and he snapped his helmet back on, tucked the severed Sploig/robot limb under one arm and hefted his linguini blaster.

"Back door?"

"Yes. And if there isn't one, make one." He nodded and started toward the back. "And see if you can raise Zook! Tell him we need transport!"

"I've got a van."

"You've got a what?" I looked at Kely like she'd sprouted wings and a halo.

"A van. You know, drab, slow, inconspicuous, full of musical instruments. A van."

"What about your band?" I had noticed that she didn't appear too emotionally crushed by the loss of her accordionist.

"Two dead, one fled. Besides, I'd only been playing with them for a week." She pulled a set of keys from a pocket that I'd not thought possible in her outfit and jingled them before my eyes. "Shall we?"

I'd rather be lucky than good any day.

"Turk, make a door. We've got a ride!"

***

Kely wasn't lying about her van: it wasn't pretty, it wasn't fast, and it was literally packed with musical instruments.

"Will this thing even fly?" I asked, removing the business end of a saxophone from between the halves of my derrière.

"Yes, and be careful with that! It's a classic!"

"A classic saxophone?"

"Yes!"

"How is there such a thing as a classic saxophone? They weren't even invented until 1840, and the inventor was a Belgian!"

"How did you know that?" She looked at me like I'd grown horns and a tail. "Nobody knows that!"

"Uh, well, I do." I wasn't about to tell her that I had a synthetic brain that just happened to have a full version of Encyclopedia Galactica on its hard drive. We weren't that close. Not yet.

"Oh, you do, do you? Well, who invented the clarinet?"

"Johann Christoph Denner."

"When?"

"1690." I couldn't help myself. The answers came out of my mouth before I could think to stop them.

"How do you know that?"

"Uh, I don't know. I just know it." Yeah, that was brilliant.

"Harry knows a lot of weird stuff," Kik said, obviously hoping to help. I don't think she was helping much, if the look that Kely gave her was any indication. "Can we just leave now, please?"

"Oh, yeah. I suppose we should." Well, at least Kely was pragmatic. The sirens were so loud now that my fillings were vibrating in perfect resonance with the pitch.

She gunned the ancient grav motor. It coughed out a plume of noxious vapor that was probably highly radioactive, and was roughly the size of the vehicle. We lurched into the air and slewed around a corner, leaving a trail of smoke that a blind Slefothian could follow.

Yes, I *know*, Slefothians don't have eyes... It was a *joke*. Jeez.

Anyway, I don't think this bucket of bolts would pass emission control on its best day, and Kely was definitely pushing it beyond its limits. I would have felt a lot safer with Kik at the controls—why are you surprised by that?—but she was busy sharing the back seat with Turk and a whole slew of instruments, most in black leather cases. I heard a creak as we rounded another corner, and you'd have thought that someone poked Kely with a cattle prod.

"Careful, damn it!" She braked sharply to avoid a kid on a Hov-R-Board™ and glared over her shoulder at Turk. "Break that violin and I'll have your testicles for earrings! It's an original Guarneri!"

"What's that?"

"A Guarneri is a violin. A very old, special, expensive violin."

"No. Not that. That!" Turk's armored hand thrust forward between the bucket seats, his index finger almost punching through the unbreakable windscreen.

Okay, so we looked.

And wished we hadn't.

"Crap!" That was me.

"Seconded!" That was Kely. Okay she won on eloquence points.

Kely swerved to miss the insane-looking vehicle that was barreling toward us at slightly less than supersonic speed. It was roughly the size of a tractor-trailer wadded into a slightly oblong ball, and the hull glowed with scintillating colors.

One guess...

"Who the hell was that?" Kely exclaimed, bringing her rattle trap van back on course with only a minor *clatter-creak-crunch* of musical paraphernalia.

"Sploig."

"Bless you. Now, who was that?"

"It wasn't a sneeze, it was a name. They're called Sploig. Those two things in the bar were Sploig, or at least were sent by the Sploig. They're trying to kill us!"

"Why?"

"Long story!"

"INCOMING!"

That, at least, she understood. At Turk's scream, she turned the van so hard that we almost hit a building. It was good that we missed, because the thing that the Sploig had shot at us didn't. A large section of the building vanished in a sizzle that made those we'd experienced in The Inferno seem like shuffling across a carpeted floor and touching a doorknob. The shockwave sent us careening out of control for half a block, and we tore through a few dozen political advertisements that were strung across the way. It was kind of hard to see through the smiling Carpoolian faces plastered against the windscreen, but Kely managed to get us back on course. Of course, that just made us that much easier to get a good bead on.

"They're right behind us!" That was Kik, and she sounded like she would also have much preferred to be at the controls.

"There!" I pointed for emphasis, figuring that it had worked for Turk, why not me?

"Where?"

I guess it didn't.

"There! The alley! It's too narrow for them!"

"Right!"

"No! Left!"

"I know!"

"Then why did you say—"

"INCOMING!"

Never was being shot at so welcome; the conversation was going nowhere.

Kely couldn't even approximate the aerobatic artistry of my pilot, but she managed to evade the incoming fire. I found out later that much of that was due to Turk's uncanny ability to gauge when and where the enemy was going to shoot—what he lacked in neurons, he made up for in raw talent. That, and the fact that he had shot out the back window of the van and was draining the power cell of his linguini blaster firing at the nose of the pursuing vehicle.

The result of their combined talent—or the lack thereof—kept us breathing for a few more minutes, but the scraping impact as we ricocheted around the corner into the alley left Kely's van even less aesthetically pleasing and even more aerodynamically impaired. The upside was that we were now shooting down an alley far too narrow for the Sploig to follow.

"Slow down. I think we're relatively safe in here." At least I hoped so. The two buildings were reasonably well built. How did I know? They were pre-Preemptive Punitive Measure construction. Anything that hadn't collapsed with the bombardment had to be relatively tough.

"So why are those things chasing you?" Kely turned into an even narrower side alley. I wasn't going to complain; it felt positively cozy.

"The story hasn't gotten any shorter. Mind if I fill you in later?"

"Mind if I drop you off at the corner?"

"Huh?" You guessed it; my suave persona had made itself known again.

"If you don't tell me why the hell those things were trying to kill you, you're out of my van before you can tell me who invented the harmonica."

"Christian Friedrich Buschmann, 1821 in Germany, and they were trying to kill us because we're after them."

"How do you know this stuff?" She glared at me, then her eyebrows shot up at the rest of what I'd said. "Hey, wait a minute; *you* are after *them*? What are you talking about?"

"They stole something that belongs to Earth, and we're trying to find it and take it back. Or maybe convince them to bring it back." She just stared. "Okay, I hadn't really gotten that far yet. I was concentrating on finding them first."

"I think you found them." She'd slowed the van to a crawl and was taking every corner she could, as long as the streets were narrow.

"Actually, I think they found us, though I can't figure out how. We hadn't even gotten any information from Neezl when they walked in and started shooting." I scratched my scalp, trying to think of where we might have left a trail. Could it have been the Farfnian Patrol boat? The cab driver? Maybe one of the port officials? Sam, the piano player? No, wait. That was the movie I'd been watching in my quarters during the long, dull string-trip here.

What, you've never seen *Casablanca*?

Are you *sure* you're human?

"So they're trying to kill you because they know you've come after them. Well, I can understand that, though I can't understand why they would be afraid of you if they have armor, weapons, and vehicles like that." She turned another corner. I was getting pretty lost.

"Maybe they know something about us that we don't."

"Make sense, Kik! What could they know about us that we don't?"

"Plenty, Harry. Remember what Zook told us about them?"

"The shape-shifting part or the time-traveling part?"

"Huh?" Well, I guess Miss Smarty Musician Lady wasn't so omniscient after all. Ha!

"Well, I was thinking about the second one, but the other thing could have been part of it."

"Who the hell are these Sploig, anyway?" Kely was starting to sound a little overwhelmed, and since she was the one driving, I thought I really did owe her an explanation.

"They're time-traveling galactic overlords who ruled the Milky Way about forty-thousand years ago and have come forward in time to steal the secret of cheese to introduce to the Farfnian home world before they come to power, thus retroactively defeating the crabs and retaining their hold on the galaxy."

"Oh. Okay."

She just stared forward and drove without twitching a muscle. She'd either blown a gasket, thought we were lunatics, or was trying to accept everything I'd just said and retain a scrap of sanity.

Yeah, right... Good luck!

The problem with telling Kely everything was that she wasn't really paying attention to where she was driving, and when we came to an intersection with a rather wide avenue, she just drove right out into it.

The good news was there wasn't much traffic.

The bad news was there was no traffic because the Sploig craft we'd dodged was sitting right there waiting for us.

"Uh-oh."

"Harry!" That was Turk, and I knew what he was going to tell me. It all made sense how he knew just when and where the Sploig were going to fire.

"I know." The forward array of sizzlers was hard to miss, and it was glowing from blue to white at an astonishing rate, emitting a low hum that had my teeth rattling in my head.

We had about a half second to live.

CHAPTER SIX

SPLOIG SANDWICH

Okay, I realize I said "a half second to live," but time seems to fly when you're having fun, and we were having just so much that we could hardly stand it, if you count watching an energy weapon that will obliterate you glow increasingly white-hot in preparation "fun".

You ever hear the term "Too much fun?"

Oh yeah, we were having that plus some.

Anyway, while we were contemplating our very brief futures, I realized why we were in such a pickle.

"They know."

"What?" That was Turk, not exactly my choice for conversation, but we were in a pinch and everyone else was a little...well...catatonic.

"They know. The Sploig. They know everything."

"Time travel."

I actually looked over my shoulder at Turk in astonishment. If there was one person in the universe who I did not expect mental leaps from, it was Turk. I didn't even expect mental stumbles from Turk. But he'd gotten it. He knew.

Fat lot of good it was going to do us seconds before we were going to be vaporized.

Then, as I was turned, looking into Turk's broad Cro-Magnon features, his eyes grew very wide. I could only think that we were about to be disintegrated, so I said a very short "Well, you're not going to get out of this one, Harry" to myself and gritted my teeth.

A roar filled the cab of the little van, a resonance so deep that every musical instrument in there with us started to...well...resonate. For a second it sounded like the St. Louis Philharmonic tuning up for an opera. Then there was a tremendous crash, and the van lurched alarmingly.

I thought we were dead.

I'd never imagined death being so...uh...lively, and from the look of utter astonishment and glee painting Turk's features—and they could use some painting, let me tell you—we weren't dead at all!

I risked looking back out the front windscreen of the van.

"Well, I'll be damned."

The nose of the *Limburger* was about two meters in front of the front bumper, the belly of the ship resting firmly upon the pavement. She was looking like her old self; that is, slightly dented. I could only assume that the Sploig vehicle was somewhere beneath it.

"Your ship?" Kely had found her vocal cords, evidently.

"Yep."

"Looks like Zook needs some more flying lessons."

I looked back at Kik. "*More* flying lessons?"

"Well, yeah. After our last trip, we both thought it would be smart to have an alternate pilot. You know, someone who could take the helm if something happened to me." She must have read the look on my face. "Not that there's anything wrong with your piloting, Harry, but you're captain. You've got, uh...captain stuff to do. You shouldn't be flying the ship."

"I see your point." I really didn't, but I thought it was nice that she was trying to spare my feelings. I think that was a first for Kik.

"You mean you're *really* the captain of that?" Kelly asked skeptically.

Before I could answer, Turk's helmet started squawking in a voice that I recognized all too readily.

"It's Zook!" Turk was back to his usual state-the-obvious self.

"Tell him to open the door."

"He says which one?"

"The airlock! He'd have to lift the ship to open the cargo bay, and while I think our Sploig friends might have a little trouble shrugging off being flattened by a five hundred-ton stringship, I wouldn't take bets on it." I looked to Kely apologetically. "You'll have to leave your van behind."

"Huh?"

"What?" That was Kik, which surprised me.

"She's coming with us?" There was an unmistakable lilt in Turk's usual baritone that I would have found amusing if I wasn't so caught off guard.

"Well, I—"

"What makes you think I'm coming with you?" Kely put the van down next to the airlock and turned to me with a quizzical scowl. Yes, I'm sure it was a quizzical scowl; I took very careful note of it.

"Well, I—"

"She gives us a ride, and you think she's going to jump into this mess with us?"

Okay, Kik has a way of putting things that always makes me feel stupid.

"Well, I—"

"She *could* come with us, if she wants to." Yep, hopeful lilt, all right. Turk was falling fast.

"Nice of you to *ask*, Turk," Kely said, her scowl losing its question mark, "but I've got classes to teach tomorrow, and another gig tomorrow night."

"You teach *classes*?" I'm so suave I astound me. Her scowl turned from neutral to accusative.

"Music and marksmanship at Carpool U. I've got Ph.D.'s in both. What's wrong with teaching classes?" She exited the van and helped Kik and Turk disentangle themselves from her musical instrumentation.

"Nothing! I just thought..."

"You just thought I was some kind of traveling tattooed-gypsy-musician-freak who would jump at the chance at having a *real* adventure with a dashing, cheese-running captain and his oddball crew."

"I'm dashing?" Well, maybe not.

"Hey! Who you callin' oddball?" Kik was managing a pretty effective scowl of her own.

That was when Zook opened the airlock door and yelled, "Hurry up, Harry! We've got crabs incoming!"

We all looked, and I had to agree with Kely; we were pretty oddball, all right. Zook was standing in the airlock door fully nude and hairless from head to toe. He'd evidently been in too big a hurry to put his clothes back on after piloting the *Limburger*. He seemed unperturbed by the fact that everyone was looking at him. I hadn't had the same poise when I'd exited the pilot's couch, but I had to admit, he looked a little better without hair than I had.

"Hmmm, maybe I *will* come along."

"Huh?" I looked at Kely, then looked where she was looking.

Okay, so Zook looked a *lot* better than I had without hair— and clothes. I guess Immortals get to choose the bodies they copy. He'd made a good choice. That was when I heard the echo of distant Farfnian security sirens headed our way. Never a sweeter sound touched my ears.

"Sorry, Kely, but we're in a bit of a hurry, now. We don't have time to load all your instruments." Well, it made a good excuse, anyway. "You should get as far away as you can before we punch out of here. I wouldn't bet that the Sploig are dead." I grabbed Turk's arm and pushed him toward the airlock. I didn't have much success, but I tried.

"Uh…yeah!" Nice to know Turk wasn't trying to match me for off-the-cuff excuses. "Uh…we gotta go!"

"Thanks for the ride!" Okay, so Kik was beating me on the polite-o-meter. I think that was a first, too. "I like your outfit, by the way."

"Yours, too!" Kelly smiled, and the two did one of those quick platonic girl-hug kind of things.

Oh, great. Girl bonding...

Dressed as they were, it should have been arousing on many levels, but at that moment, I found it rather absurd. Go figure.

I pushed Turk harder, and he actually started moving.

"If you're ever on Earth, look us up! Bye now! Take care! Drive carefully!"

Thankfully, she just stood there and waved. Responding in any way to my inane drivel would have only encouraged my poor overtaxed prosthesis to come up with more of the same. We crowded into the airlock with Zook—Uncomfortable? Well, duh!—and he cycled the inner door open.

"Sorry about the last-minute rescue, Harry," he said, leading the way to the bridge amid several stares of shock and admiration from the crew. "I was flying by the seat of my...uh..." He stopped and looked down at himself, and gave us one of those absent-minded professor grins that make him so lovable and utterly alien.

"Well, anyway, I got Turk's call for help, and I didn't think a cab would do you much good. Not with Sploig chasing you."

"Which brings up the question, how did you do it?"

"How did I do what?"

Now that caught me off guard; I had actually stumped the wellspring of all one-upmanship? I was speechless. Which made it that much more difficult to carry on a conversation.

"I think he means, how did you beat the Sploig to the punch?"

I would have to thank Turk later...damn it.

"Oh, that."

"Yeah, that." We got into the lift and I pushed the button that would take us to the bridge. "They'd been one step ahead of us since we walked into The Inferno. They knew exactly when and where we were going to meet with Neezl. They shot him right before he told us about them. They knew we hitched a ride, and with whom, where we were going to run, and how we were going to evade them. Then when we did, they knew where we'd pop up."

"Time travel," Turk put in, just trying to help.

"Yes, well, there are certain things they know, and certain things they do not know. You know?"

"No," all three of us said in perfect unison.

"Well," he said, just as the lift doors opened, "we Immortals have an old saying: 'Never try to second-guess a Sploig.'"

"And that means?"

"You've got to skip to third-, fourth- or fifth-guessing them."

"Ah. Of course." The three of us just stared at him.

"Think of it this way: If your actions are consistently unpredictable—that is, random or spur of the moment—you may well react to identical situations differently on two separate occasions or time lines."

More blank stares.

"Think of it in terms of chaos theory."

I was almost sure that wouldn't help, but I tried. "Okay..."

"If there are enough random variables to an equation, variables that change every time you solve the equation, you'll never get the same answer twice."

"Okay..."

"So if I take enough variables into consideration every time I make a decision, they won't be able to predict me, either."

"Uh, Harry?"

"Yes, Turk?"

"I know this is interesting and all, but," he made an impatient gesture with his eyebrows, then gave a pointed stare at Zook, "aren't we a little rushed?"

"Oh, yeah." I'd let myself get caught up, always a danger with Zook. "I think it would be best if we discussed it later, Zook. Kik, Turk, let's get out of here. Zook, would you put some clothes on, please?"

"Sure, Harry," they all chimed, turning to their duties.

Nice to know I was still captain, at least.

Turk went to tactical, Zook picked up his jumper and started putting it on, and Kik started disentangling herself from her fringe. I managed to get to my seat without tripping over my tongue and punched up the viewer.

"Looks like Kely's on her way," I said, plugging myself in as Kik closed the lid to the pilot's couch. The vid picked up Kely's beat-up old van heading up the same alley we'd come out of. "Are the lifters on line?"

"Sure," Kik responded in my head. The drone of the lift engines was enough to tell me my question was redundant. "How high?"

"How close are they, Turk?"

"Just a few blocks. And they've called in the big boys, too. There's a light cruiser on a steep descent. About forty seconds and he'll be parked on top of us."

"Zook, I think it's time for our disappearing stringship trick."

"The field's already shaping up, Harry. Just get us some altitude and get clear of the buildings."

I relayed that to Kik, making it sound like it was my idea, of course.

"No problem, Harry."

The *Limburger* left the ground with a screech of tortured metal and a few clanks and clatters. I'd forgotten about the Sploig we'd splattered. They better not have dented my ship!

"Is she spaceworthy, Zook?"

"I have no idea, Harry, but it should be interesting if she isn't."

I gave him The Look.

He gave me The Smile.

Jeez, he creeps me out!

"Well, I guess there's only one way to find out, isn't there? Just tell me when we're clear, Zook."

"Just about...now!"

"Kik, shift us into stringspace, please." I was trying for nonchalant. What the hell. If we exploded, at least...uh...I was trying to think of a bright side of the ship exploding when I felt the familiar jolt of the shift, and the front view screen went black.

No explosion.

"Hm, well, there you go. She's spaceworthy, I guess." My nonchalance was getting a little stressed.

"Well, we don't really know that, do we, Harry?" Zook gave me The Smile again. "We're not technically *in* space, are we?"

He had me there; you could strap string-engines onto my Aunt Petunia's backside and shift her into stringspace. That didn't make her a stringship, although her backside *did* exceed the minimum legal dimensions for a commercial ship. And no I am not exaggerating; Aunt Petunia's slightly...gravity challenged.

"Well, then I guess we just better make sure she is spaceworthy before we shift back into normal space, hadn't we? You wanna get started on that, Zook?"

"Sure, Harry." He sauntered off the bridge, and yes, I'm quite sure it was a saunter.

Arrogant Immortals...humph.

I keyed open the shipwide and said, "We're in stringspace again, so you can all relax for a while. Everyone have a look around your sections and report any damage to the bridge."

"Uh, Harry?" That was Kik, and she was still in my head. She hadn't come out of the couch yet.

"Something wrong, Kik?"

"Nothing really. I just wondered if you could scrounge me up a jumper or something. I don't feel like putting the outfit back on. You know."

"Sure, Kik. I understand." Actually, I didn't understand at all. Kik was about as modest as I was religious. What next, Turk quoting Tolstoy? "I'd loan you mine, but it's a little dirty."

I looked around the bridge, but there was nothing even resembling clothing lying amongst the clutter. The closest I could come up with was two disk cases and a Band-Aid®, unless she'd settle for being covered in Jiffy Whip™, but that would be just way too tempting, and I was on a diet, so...

"Turk, you got a spare jumper or something in the weapons locker for Kik? She doesn't think that club-wear is exactly appropriate for the occasion."

"I think so, hang on." He rummaged through the locker, piling an inordinate amount of ordinance on the deck, and finally came up with an extra-extra-extra-large lime-green jump suit that was only slightly rumpled. Obviously it was one of Turk's spares. It would fit Kik like a tent fits a ballerina, but it would cover everything, so...

"Okay, Kik, Turk has an extra jumper. It's a little large, but it'll do until you get to your quarters."

"Thanks, Harry." The pilot's couch cycled open and she stepped out, accepting the garment from Turk and slipping into its voluminous folds. I busied my eyes elsewhere, and when I looked back she was clothed.

"You look like Gumby® after a low-spin cycle." So suave, yet so stupid... Yeah.

"Thanks!" She finished rolling up a sleeve and snatched up her club outfit. It fit nicely into one of the jumper's pockets. "I'm going to get changed."

She tried to swagger to the lift, but the jumper's crotch hit her just about at the knees. She took three steps and almost tripped, while I bit my lip to keep from laughing. Turk had less success, and the glare she threw at him would have melted hull metal. The swagger devolved into a shuffle and she vanished into the lift, sweeping the bridge with one more caustic glare.

There were no casualties.

"Well, I think I could do with a change of clothing, too," I said, standing and brushing at some of the slime and grime on my jumper.

"And maybe a shower?" Turk asked as he started disassembling his assault armor. It had sustained a few scratches, and he'd probably be up all night ironing them out.

"Uh, yeah." I sniffed...not a good idea when you're covered with Carpoolian. "Not a bad idea, and since we've got plenty of time, I think I'll—"

That, of course, was the cue for the communications panel to bleep for attention. I really should know better.

"Fische here," I said after stabbing the button.

"Harry, it's Charley. I think you should come down here."

"Here where?" I asked. He could have been in the head for all I knew. Oh, come on! It's a ship! A "head" is a bathroom!

"The main hold." There was a dramatic pause. "We've got a problem."

"What kind of problem, Charley? Give me some specifics!" I hate it when people keep me in the dark because they're afraid I'm going to yell at them. I mean, I never yell. I'm the epitome of cool-headedness in all situations. I exude calm at all times.

Yeah, okay, so I'm overdoing it, but appearances are more important than facts. Ask any politician.

"There's a weird-looking vehicle smashed up through the landing platform, the hatch is open, and there are greasy-looking, three-toed footprints leading away from the wreckage. Specific enough?"

"Uh, yeah." Calm, I'm calm. "Thanks Charley." I am the epitome of cool-headedness. "I'll be right down."

I turned off the intercom.

"Turk?" Calm....

"Yes, Harry?"

"Could I maybe borrow a weapon from your collection?" Serene... I am utterly calm...

"What kind would you like, Harry?"

"I want the biggest (expletive deleted) gun you've got that won't blow the ship to (expletive deleted) smithereens if I (expletive deleted) up, okay?" Yes...calm...serene...male bovine excrement... You get the picture.

"How about this?" He held out something that looked like a satellite dish mounted on a Cuisinart™.

"Perfect." I had no idea what it was, but under these circumstances, I trusted Turk implicitly.

He handed it to me and I looked it over.

"Only one question."

"What's that, Harry?" he asked as he started buckling on his only recently discarded assault armor.

"Which is the dangerous end?"

"Here." He took it and put it into my hands, the dish pointing away from me. "Just point the dish in the general direction of anything you don't like. Push the little stud there, and it'll get cooked."

"Hmmm... Nice."

"It's one of my favorites."

"One more question?"

"Yeah?"

"You think we've got a chance in hell?"

"Against who knows how many shape-changing Sploig who have infiltrated our ship and taken the form of anyone or anything aboard?"

"Yeah, that."

"Nope."

"Just thought I'd ask." As he finished buckling on his gear and grabbed his linguini blaster, I thumbed the shipwide intercom.

"All personnel, this is Captain Fische. Code Mozzarella. I repeat, Code Mozzarella."

That was cheese runner lingo for "Grab a weapon and cover your..." Well, you get the picture.

We boarded the lift, charged our weapons and hit the button that would take us to the main hold, loaded for Sploig.

CHAPTER SEVEN

A SPLOIG IN THE HAND

I'd like to say Turk and I burst into the loading dock, guns blazing, and wiped out the evil aliens in one Sploig-cleansing surge of testosterone, but that's not exactly how it happened.

The Sploig, as usual, were one step ahead of us.

The lift stopped just about halfway to the loading dock.

The doors didn't open, the bell didn't go *ding!*, and the little electronic voice didn't say "Loading dock, level one, have a nice day."

Okay, we don't have a little electronic voice on our lift, and we've only got four levels on the *Limburger* anyway, so I don't even know why we have a lift, but it beats taking the stairs. At least it did until I got stuck in it with Turk.

"What the hell?" That was Turk, though I have to admit I was thinking the same thing.

"Maybe the damage knocked the lift out of alignment." I didn't really think so, but I didn't want Turk panicking in a five-foot-square lift.

"Or maybe the Sploig killed the power and we're trapped in here!"

Okay, that was a possibility I'd considered, but I didn't want to lend any credence to a theory that we couldn't confirm. Yeah...that's right. Because unconfirmed credence has always been a pet peeve of mine.

"Or Zook could have shut down the lift to try to keep the Sploig contained." Yes, I liked that theory much better.

"Or Zook could have heard your 'Code Mozzarella' and thought 'Oh, what fun!' and skipped off right into the Sploig's hands, in which case, if we see him we're going to have to vaporize him, because he won't be Zook, but a Sploig!"

"Or Mishi could have made his infamous supernova chili for lunch, and the demand on the ship's plumbing has overtaxed the main computer, which shut down the lift to conserve memory."

"Oh, come on, Harry. What are the chances of that happening twice in one month?"

"Not very high, I'll admit, but it *could* happen."

We stared at one another for a short while.

Turk fidgeted.

I tapped my foot.

Somewhere, a dog barked.

Did I say I *heard* a dog bark? No. I just said one did. There are billions of dogs in the universe and it is a statistical certainty that one of them was barking at that particular moment. So there!

"So what do we do, Harry?"

"Well, we could try the intercom." I poked the button. Nothing. "Or maybe not."

"We could blast our way out and climb up to the closest deck," he suggested, leveling his linguini blaster at the lift doors and thumbing the noodle that powered up the weapon. A low hum filled the lift.

"Or we could nix that idea on the grounds that your captain is not wearing assault armor and would probably be singed by bits of red-hot flying metal if you pulled that trigger, or whatever it is you pull on that thing."

"Oh, yeah." He powered down, and my sphincter tone returned to normal. Whew. "Sorry about that, Harry. I wasn't thinking."

"And that's new...how?"

Okay, that was just plain stupid. I mean, here I am stuck in a five-foot-square box with a gorilla who could snap every bone in my body without breaking a sweat, and I insult him. Who says natural selection isn't working?

Okay, maybe it isn't working; I'm alive, aren't I?

Fortunately, all Turk did was glare at me and say, "So what's *your* suggestion?"

"Well..." I had to think fast on this one or look even dumber, a seemingly difficult task considering how dumb I looked already, but one which I felt eminently qualified to perform. "How about using that narrow-beam setting that you used to cut off the Sploig robot-thing's leg. Can you cut a hole in the floor so we can climb down?"

"Climb down what?"

"Aren't there cables or access ladders or something?" The elevator shafts in the movies always have them.

"I have no idea. I've never seen inside a lift shaft before."

"Well, this is your chance."

"What if the lift is held up by a grav plate in the floor, and I ruin it when I cut through?"

"Then we fall two floors screaming, I probably break my legs, and you have to carry me around for the rest of the day, or at least until I can get to a medical kit."

"That doesn't sound so bad."

It sounded plenty bad to me, but I didn't want to look like a chicken. I mean, a *real* man should be able to take a few broken bones without crying like a baby, shouldn't he? When I find one, I'll let you know.

"Then fire away," I said, backing into the corner and trying not to cluck. "But turn that thing down so you don't cut right through the hull."

"Oh, yeah. Good idea." He fiddled his linguini, and I tried to look confident in his ability not to blow the whole ship to tiny little fragments of molten metal that would drift through stringspace until the end of the universe. Actually, if you put it that way, it sounded rather peaceful. Kind of like a really, really long vacation at an all-inclusive resort. No worries, no deadlines, no bosses, no Farfnians, and certainly no Sploig.

But there was that whole dying thing, which I've been trying really hard all my life to put off.

Call me a procrastinator.

Turk took aim at the floor and fired. I didn't see how he could miss, so I closed my eyes against the glare. The air stank of ozone and the cutting beam sounded like a violin solo being played at ten times normal speed, but the discomfort was relatively brief.

Turk stopped firing, and the subsequent silence was punctuated by the loud clang of a piece of flooring falling two floors. Well, it could have been worse; it could have been us.

I opened my eyes.

There was a lot of smoke, but there was also a Turk-sized hole in the floor. That meant Turk could fit through, but not both of us at the same time, so naturally I exerted my duty as captain and commander of my vessel.

"You first."

Turk looked at me like I'd told him he'd won the lottery. He lives for this macho crap, so I figured I'd let him have his fun.

"Right." He dropped to the floor of the lift and poked his head fearlessly through the hole he'd cut. "Looks clear, and you were right. There are four tracks that the car rides on. Shouldn't be hard to climb down. The floor of the shaft's only about seven meters."

"Great. Go ahead. I'll be right behind you."

"Right."

Turk slung his linguini over his shoulder by one noodle and scrambled through the hole like a metal-plated orangutan. I heard several *clanks* and *clatters*, then finally a solid *thump*.

"Okay, Harry, I'm down."

I tried to emulate my tin-plated friend, figuring if he could do it wearing assault armor, I should be able to do it carrying nothing but a dangerous-looking Cuisinart™. I really should make a career of being wrong; I'm very good at it. Well, at least I discovered something in being wrong: it's not the fall that hurts, it's the sudden stop at the bottom. That and landing on the business end of a Cuisinart™.

"You okay, Harry?"

I would have answered except for two things: First, pain hurts me and causes my vocal cords to constrict involuntarily. Second, I was too busy pointing up and making inarticulate sounds of exclamation to form words.

Fortunately, Turk understands this form of communication very well. He looked up.

"Oh, crap."

Yeah, that's what I had been trying to say.

The lift had resumed a rapid downward course, and was just about to make us a very flat captain and tin soldier. Fortunately for me, I was stuck at the bottom of a lift shaft with a very strong tin soldier wearing powered assault armor. Turk simply put up his arms and caught the lift, or at least tried to. His elbows buckled, and he caught it more with his face than anything else, but he did stop its downward progress.

I breathed a sigh of relief. Then Turk said something, which jarred me out of my lassitude. I'm not really sure what he said, since it's rather hard to talk with your mouth full of elevator, but it was something like, "Gahh baaa ih ahh shuuu ih daau!" (see translation #1 at the end of this transcript)

I didn't speak whatever language he'd reverted to—amazing what an impact to the head can do, isn't it?—but I did notice that the control panel inside the lift was lit up again. I hopped up and scrambled through the hole, listening to the grinding motors of the lift competing with the whining servos of Turk's powered armor. It only took a second to smack the emergency stop button, which was good, because I think the lift was winning. When I looked back down through the hole in the floor, Turk's armor was rather crinkled at the knees, though he was still standing.

"Okay, Turk. You can relax, the lift is stopped."

He didn't relax so much as collapse, but he managed to crawl up and hoist himself back into the lift.

We were right back where we started, my backside and Turk's face both only a little worse for wear, although I think my backside took the most damage by comparison. But then, it started out with more to lose than Turk's face.

At that moment, I couldn't help but think that somewhere on my ship, a Sploig was laughing.

Once Turk was fully back in, I released the stop button and the lift settled gently to the cargo deck. The doors opened with an all-too-cheerful *ding!*, and Charley and three other cargo handlers stood there, weapons trained on us, ready to blast us into Sploigettes.

"Hold on there, boys!" Charley said, raising a hand and pointing his weapon elsewhere. "It's Harry and Turk, but what the hell happened to the lift?"

"Long story," I said, working myself gingerly to my feet and making an attempt to help Turk to his. He was even shakier than I was, though part of that could have been the damage to his armor. He was moving like a puppet with too many joints. "Has anyone seen our guests?"

"How would we know if we had, Harry?" Charley and his crew helped us out of the lift and directed their small arsenal at what was left of our cargo bay. "They could be anywhere and look like anything, right?"

"Good point." Then I noticed the Sploig vehicle that had been jammed up through the hull of my ship. "Holy crap! Would you look at that!"

It was barely dented.

Well, it had a few scratches, and the sizzler array was trashed, but the hull was miraculously un-flattened. Those Sploig build tough stuff!

"It's something, isn't it?" Charley agreed, helping Turk to sit. He was mumbling something about helping him out of his armor, which the other handlers seemed willing to do. I couldn't take my eyes off the dented Sploigmobile—I didn't know what else to call it.

"You sure they're all out of it?" I took a step forward, wondering what treasures lurked inside. Heck, the whole thing was a treasure! If we could bring this back to Earth to be torn apart and analyzed, it might put us right up there with the Farfnians.

"You think I'm dumb enough to set foot in that thing?" Charley scoffed. "Just because I haul cargo for a living doesn't mean I'm stupid!"

"Well, we have to make sure there aren't more Sploig hiding in it, anyway." I didn't want to argue with him, more from the fear of losing an argument with a cargo handler than actually making him mad. But I had to agree on one count: if I was going to poke my head into an alien minivan, I wanted the biggest, baddest blaster in the universe backing me up. "How are you feeling, Turk?"

"I'm okay. The armor was pinching me is all. Saved our lives, but it got a little crumpled." He toed the pile of tortured metal, sounding like he'd lost a favored pet. "Damn shame. Good armor's hard to find."

"Bag me a couple of Sploig and I'll buy you a brand-new set. I promise."

"They're as good as bagged, Harry," he assured me, standing somewhat shakily and hefting his linguini blaster. He thumbed a noodle and the thing started humming. "Just find 'em for me."

"You said there were footprints, Charley?"

"Well, something that looked like footprints, anyway. Over here." He led us around to the other side of the craft, skirting the shards and shreds of hull metal where it had been peeled back like an orange rind. "There. Look there."

There were three rows of odd little splotchy patches on the floor. They looked wet and kind of silvery. What caught my eye even more, however, was the gaping aperture in the side of the Sploigmobile. There was no door, just a hole about a meter across and one and a half high. If this was any indication of Sploig dimensions, they weren't very big. Not that it really mattered. I've been told time and time again that size isn't important—yeah, right. Call me naive, but I'd much rather be hunting something smaller than myself than something, say, Turk-sized. And I suppose since the Sploig were shape changers that any size was their size, unless they had to conserve mass and, therefore, size as they shifted form. But then, they might be able to shift density, as well.

My scalp was starting to feel pretty warm, so I changed tactics. Too much thinking is bad for you in situations like this. While you're working your grey matter, or software in my case, something slightly less cognitive is likely to sneak up behind you and dent your CPU with a Louisville Slugger™.

I looked at the odd little prints, one small and two larger. The moisture looked like sparkly hair gel. Maybe it was Sploig blood. Maybe it was Sploig sweat. Maybe it was Sploig...um...well, suffice to say, it could have been anything, and I wasn't about to taste, touch or otherwise try to analyze it.

The aperture in the Sploigmobile led into an interior of glossy black stuff in flowing forms that struck me as utterly alien. It bore no resemblance to anything I'd ever seen before. I had no clue what to do.

There was only one thing I could think that might help, but it scared the waffles right out of me to even consider it.

"We need Zook."

There, I said it. I confronted my fear and I felt much better for it.

"Someone want to call up to engineering and ask him to come down here?"

"Don't you think we should send a security squad to bring him, Harry?"

Damn, I hate it when Turk is right.

"Oh, okay. Tell them to make sure it's him, though. In fact, tell everyone not to go anywhere alone. We might have more than one Sploig aboard, but my guess is they'll try to assume the form some of the crew. That'll be harder if everyone travels in pairs."

"Right." He promptly turned and walked off by himself to find an intercom.

"Um, Turk."

"Yeah, Harry?"

"The not-being-alone thing. That applies to you, too."

"Oh. Yeah. Sorry." He motioned one of the handlers to accompany him, and the two disappeared around the curve of the Sploigmobile. I was beginning to think that lift had done more damage than I'd first guessed.

I walked around the wrecked vehicle while we waited, though there wasn't much to see. It wasn't scintillating with color any more, of course. That must have been some kind of energy shielding or something. Now that it was turned off, it was just a dull grey. Curiosity finally got the better of me and I reached out and touched it; it felt slightly spongy. It certainly didn't feel like metal.

"Looks like you gave it one hell of a headache, at least," a sultry feminine voice said right behind me.

I must have jumped three feet in the air. And what was worse than being scared out of my wits? When I came down, Kik was laughing at me.

"Jeez! Sorry, Harry, but you should have seen yourself. You moved like I'd poked you with a cattle prod. I swear, you must have jumped three feet!

See? I wasn't exaggerating.

I wasn't laughing either.

"What are you doing wandering down here alone, Kik?" I demanded, using my best captain voice, which hadn't ever impressed her much anyway. Now, I know what you're thinking and I was thinking it, too, but I don't *always* fixate on what she's wearing, so just forget it, I'm not telling you!

That's *not* what you were thinking?

Oh, well, in that case, she was wearing her standard work jumper, no shoes, which wasn't surprising, and a pair of laser pistols. So what *were* you thinking?

Fine, don't tell me.

Anyway, after her amusement subsided to the point where she could breathe again, Kik said, "You kidding? After your 'Code Mozzarella,' I wasn't going to sit in my cabin alone! I went to the bridge, but there was nobody there." She shrugged, nodding to the gun in my hands. "Why the call to arms, anyway?"

"We've got Sploig aboard, Kik. Or didn't you notice the vehicle jammed up through our cargo hold floor?"

"Really? They survived?" She started looking around with a peculiar glint in her eye that I recognized immediately.

"Don't even think it, Kik!"

"Why not, Harry? I mean, think about it!" She fingered the zipper pull of her jumper, her hottiness turned on full blast. "I mean, they're *shape*-changers, right?"

"No, Kik. They tried to kill us, remember?"

"So what better way to patch up relations than to—"

"No, Kik."

"But what would be the harm in—"

"No, Kik."

"Not even—"

"No, Kik." I relaxed a little. Yep, it was her all right.

What? Of *course* I thought she might be a Sploig! You think I slipped a chip or something? But she'd passed my little quiz; not even a shape-shifting alien could mimic Kik's warped sense of...well...stuff.

"So where are they?" she asked in full pout mode.

"We don't know where they are."

"Well, then you probably shouldn't walk around alone, should you?" She gave me that I-told-you-so look that was so familiar I barely noticed it.

"Charley and the others are just around the other side of the—"

"Freeze, Sploig!"

I whirled at Turk's distinctive bellow and found his linguini blaster pointed right at us. I wanted to intervene before he made a horrible mistake and vaporized my pilot, not that I hadn't wanted to do the same occasionally. I stepped in front of Kik and said, "Hold on there, Turk. That's really Kik. I tested her already."

"Not her, Sploig, you! Drop the weapon!"

"Huh?" I looked behind us, but there was no weapon-toting Sploig hiding there.

That was when I walked out from behind Turk and said, "Careful, Turk. Don't hit Kik!"

I looked at me and blinked.

At first I thought my brain had glitched, then it all came together: who better to impersonate than the captain? I had no doubt in my mind who the Sploig was, but it's not often you see yourself giving your security officer orders to be careful while killing you. Not that I was savoring the moment; I was just too dumbfounded to say anything.

"Wait, Turk. Don't shoot!" Kik stepped in front of me then, and I could have kissed her. I don't doubt for a second that she saved my life.

"Thanks, Kik. I—"

"Shut up, Sploig," she said, leveling a laser at my chest.

"But Kik, I'm really Harry!" Yes I *did* expect her to believe me! Why not?

"Sure you are." Her pistol didn't twitch a millimeter.

Okay, so maybe not.

"Oh, this is ridiculous! Kik, get out of the way so Turk can blast the thing!" Yeah, that was me. Not *me*, the other me. I guess neither of us are very good at judging her. I could see the temper smoldering in her eyes even before she turned and gave him both barrels, verbally of course.

"Harry, I'm taking this Sploig prisoner, so don't you try to kill him! We can't learn anything from them if we just blast him to bits!"

"No, Kik. They tried to kill us, remember?"

"So what better way to patch up relations than to—"

"No, Kik."

"But what would be the harm in—"

"No, Kik."

"Not even—"

"No, Kik."

I was either having the most amazing déjà vu, or this Sploig was more like me than I was, which was equally disturbing.

That was when the lift gave another cheerful *ding!*, and a third party entered the scene. I almost expected to see another me walk out of the doors, so you can imagine my relief when three armored security guards and Zook emerged.

"Now *this* is *really* interesting!" he said, that quirky smile of his in full form.

CHAPTER EIGHT

ME²

I looked at me and glared.

I glared right back at me.

Don't get me wrong; I don't really dislike the way I look, although I usually prefer a mirror for the purpose of self-inspection. To me, he—the other me—looked like he had his hair parted on the wrong side. I liked it better my way. The other me had his microwave Cuisinart™ pointed in my direction. With my luck *he* could actually *use* the thing. The only thing keeping him from pulling the trigger was Kik, bless her horny little heart. Of course, she was pointing a gun at me, too.

Well, I couldn't disagree with Zook; this was certainly interesting, if somewhat freaky, totally frightening, and about as comfortable as congress with a porcupine. Not that I ever... Oh, it's an analogy, for cripes sake!

I wondered briefly how the Sploig had pulled it off. I mean, I couldn't have been out of sight of Charley and the others for more than a few seconds, a minute at the most. It must have been right there in front of us, maybe pretending to be a bit of twisted metal or floor plating. It had to have changed form in a split second, watching the others until nobody's attention was on it, and then blinking into my shape in a heartbeat.

Quite a party trick.

But just because it looked like me, didn't mean it *was* me!

"I'm me and I can prove it!" I challenged, looking from face to face, none of which were particularly friendly.

"Oh, this ought to be good!" Charley said with a snort of laughter. "The real Harry was with us the whole time!"

I reminded myself to dock his pay.

"Okay," I began, smiling confidently. That was my first mistake. "You and I had a conversation about cargo before we left Turp Prime, Charley. Do you remember it?"

"Of course I do. But the conversation was with *him*, not you."

"Then ask him if he knows how many cans of air freshener we brought onboard."

"Fifty cans of air freshener, twenty cases of nose plugs, fifty extra gas masks, and twelve hundred scented pine trees," the Sploig said without missing a beat.

"That's exactly right," Charley corroborated.

I was in deep trouble.

"Oh, sure! It must have gotten a look at the manifest! But what did I tell him to do with the scented pine trees?"

"Hang them on our rearview mirrors," the Sploig said.

"Ha! Wrong! I said hang them on our doorknobs!" I countered.

"He said both." Charley took a step back from the Sploig-me and started looking nervously at first one of us, then the other. "How did you know that?" he asked.

"Good question," both of us said as if on cue. We glared, and then said, "How *did* you know that?" Then, "Stop that!"

"Well, I think that is enough Twenty Questions," Zook said, grinning that savant grin of his. I wondered if the Sploig-me was just as creeped out. "All this proves is that we've had a stowaway for some time, which is really no big surprise."

"It's not?" Turk's face was flushing a little, and the muzzle of his linguini blaster was wavering between the two of me. "It's a (expletive deleted) surprise to me!"

"Which also is no surprise," Zook continued. I guess he didn't mind getting his arm broken. "Right now, I think the most important thing is for both of you Harrys to drop your guns before someone gets hurt."

"Sure," I said, dropping the microwave Cuisinart™.

"Fine," the other me said, doing the same.

"Now *that* is interesting!" Zook strode between us and looked closely at the two fallen firearms. He toed mine, rolling it over, then did the same to the other one. "Very interesting!"

"I don't get it," Turk said, pointing his linguini at the deck to avoid Zook, who had walked right into his line of fire. "What's so interesting?"

"Simple, my short-sighted friend: how many of this particular type of gun do we have onboard?"

"Only one, but… Holy crap!"

"Indeed!" Zook waved his hands at the two weapons. "One of these isn't real."

"You mean one of these is a Sploig?" Kik asked, taking a half step back from me and my fallen Cuisinart™.

"Or part of a Sploig. They're either able to split into pieces, or they're communal and can form together into a larger whole." Zook was so engrossed in his examination of the two weapons that he didn't see the other me take a slow step to his left.

I was watching it, however, and shouted, "Don't let that Sploig get away, Charley!"

"Don't be ridiculous!" the Sploig countered, pointing an accusative finger at me. "It's trying to take your attention off of it so it can run!"

The muzzles of every weapon in the crowd swayed first toward me, then toward the other me. They settled out about fifty-fifty, which meant I'd gained some credibility. Probably more than I'd ever had with *this* crew.

"So what do we do?" Charley asked, squinting at first one of us, then the other.

"Well we can't shoot both of them, I guess." Turk sounded way too disappointed to make me feel particularly safe. "Can we?"

"No, you can't!" both of us chimed, in perfect chorus.

"Wait a second," Kik said, waving her laser pistol back and forth like a wagging finger. "With Harry's prosthetic brain it should be easy to tell them apart!"

"It should?" Turk scratched his forehead where the elevator had left a dent.

"Sure! Watch." She thought for a second and asked. "Okay, Harrys, who invented the harmonica!"

"Joseph Richter!" I chimed.

"Wrong! Christian Friederich Ludwig Buschmann!" the Sploig countered.

"No, *you're* wrong! Ricther invented the two-tone reed system, and the—"

"Two-tone my ass! Bushemann was the inventor. Richter just modified—"

"Both of you, shut up!" Turk bellowed.

We shut up and glared at one another. I guess neither of us was stupid enough to argue with a twitchy, brain-damaged security chief with a handful of nuclear-powered pasta.

"Well, which is right?" he asked Zook, looking like he wanted to shoot something and just waiting for the word 'fire'.

"How should I know?"

Everyone looked at Zook, including the Sploig and me, but just for a second before they pointed their weapons back at us. That was the first time I'd ever heard Zook admit to not knowing something and I was taken rather aback by it. I mean, he's an Immortal! They're supposed to know *everything*.

"What do you mean you don't know?" Kik evidently had the same misconception regarding Immortals as I did.

"I know a great many things, Kikira, but musical trivia is not a category in which I excel. I do, however, know a bit of mathematics, which I think our captain might be a bit faster with than our guest."

"Math?" Turk asked, frowning, probably at the idea that math could do *anything*, let alone tell the two Harrys apart.

"Yes, Turk. For instance," and here he began to speak very quickly, "how many minutes would it take an ellipsoid tank with perpendicular diameters of one meter and point five meters, which is half full of water and oriented with its longer axis vertically, to drain out of a hole two centimeters in diameter, assuming no planetary spin effect and a gravity of exactly one point two gee?

"Four minutes twenty-four seconds," we both said in perfect synchrony.

Crap.

Now *that* was scary and even Zook's eyebrows arched at the speed with which we'd both answered. Now, I know I've got a computer for a brain, but I didn't think the Sploig could duplicate me that accurately.

"Interesting!" I'm not even going to let you guess who that was.

Then the answer hit me. It knew the answer, because it had known the question before the question had been asked.

"Time travel," I said, finally beating the Sploig to the punch.

"Or it's reproduced my brain as well as my body," it counterpunched.

"There are a good many paradoxes lurking in the time-travel explanation," Zook hypothesized. "For instance, if the Sploig knew the question I would ask, they would also have known I would drop the *Limburger* on their vehicle, yet did nothing to prevent it. It also means they will survive this encounter, at least one of them, to travel back to their time to impart the information that they already knew when they got here."

"Huh?"

That was virtually everybody else in the cargo bay, except for Turk, who I think had drifted off to sleep for a moment.

"Quite an interesting predicament, wouldn't you say, Harry?" Zook was having way too much fun with this.

"Quite," we both agreed in perfect unison.

"I still think we should shoot them both and sort it out later," Turk muttered just loud enough for both of us to hear.

"Actually, Turk, I think you have come up with the best idea yet."

"Huh?"

"And I think we should use these!" Zook bent and picked up the gun I'd dropped and handed it to Charley, then picked up the one the Sploig had dropped and handed it to Kik. "Kik, I want you to shoot this Harry," he said, nodding to me, "and Charley, you shoot that Harry. One…two…"

"*Wait!*"

Strangely, that was Kik and Charley chiming into to the Me Chorus.

"You want to shoot *both* of us?" I asked incredulously.

"What do you think *that* will accomplish?" the other me demanded.

"Actually, I don't believe the Sploig who has assumed the shape of one of these two guns can really function as a gun, so, in fact, only one of you will be shot, and you should have noticed that I switched the weapons, so the real Harry's gun is now pointing at the Sploig Harry, by default." He smiled, obviously very satisfied with his deduction.

"And what about the theory that the Sploig could mimic my prosthetic brain, Zook?" I asked.

"If it can mimic an Immortal's computer, it can mimic a dangerous-looking Cuisinart™!" the other me added, obviously trying to save its own skin, since my real gun was now pointed at it.

"Shut up, Sploig!" Turk said, waving his linguini at the two of us.

"I am *so* going to demote your butt when this is over, Turk!"

Regretfully, the Sploig beat me to the punch on that one. Well, I was thinking it, anyway.

"Please be quiet, Harrys," Zook said without a hint of rancor. "You have no say in this. Now, what did you two want?" he asked Kik and Charley.

"Uh, I just wanted to know if we shoot on three or if you were going to say 'fire' or something." Charley seemed utterly unconcerned with the prospect of vaporizing his employer. Yep, he was definitely going to get a pay cut.

"I wanted to know what we were going to do if both guns work and we kill Harry?" Kik, at least, seemed minimally concerned.

"Well, I didn't really think of that," Zook admitted, scratching his chin.

Pay cut.

"But I'm quite sure that won't happen. So fire on 'fire', okay?"

"Sure," Kik said.

"Got it," Charley said.

"No it's (expletive deleted) not okay!" both of me shouted, edging away from the dish-shaped weapons.

"No complaining, Harry. You'll be fine. Now, one… two…three…"

Several things happened before Zook could say "fire," none of them good.

First, I was looking right at Kik when the Cuisinart™ in her hands changed so fast that I thought I was hallucinating. One second she had a gun trained on me, and the next a big puddle of silvery stuff liquefied in her hands. Before she could even scream, it slithered down the neck of her jumper.

That was when the other me went to pieces.

No, I don't mean he had a nervous breakdown, I mean, he actually came apart. The Sploig split into four roughly equal pieces: head and left arm, right arm and the rest of my chest, and each leg with a portion of abdomen. And if that were not horrifying enough, as each piece of me hit the floor, it sprouted dozens of odd little spider appendages and started skittering away.

Kik screamed, thrashing at her jumper.

I tried to grab Kik, not sure how or even if I could help.

Turk waved his linguini blaster indecisively.

Charley shouted something about deified excrement and backpedaled.

Zook just watched.

And the really bad part hadn't even happened yet!

When the four pieces of the Sploig started skittering across the deck in four different directions, gaining speed quickly, Turk's few functioning neurons must have finally made contact with one another, taken a vote, and decided that any dead Sploig was a good Sploig. When he fired, the bit of Sploig was about four feet away from me, behind Kik. Naturally, the Sploig was vaporized—Turk can usually hit what he is aiming at. Unfortunately, the deck was underneath the annihilated alien, and a large portion of it was also vaporized.

The odd thing was, I didn't notice.

I was too busy trying to get Kik out of her jumper.

If you're thinking this was an odd time for me to be doing such a thing, please consider that she was screaming "Get it off!" repeatedly. I knew she meant the Sploig, not her jumper, but since the Sploig was *under* her jumper...well, first things first.

As Kik and I both struggled to remove the garment—not as arousing an activity as you might think, under the circumstances— all I could think was if I ever got my hands on the inventor of the zipper—Whitcomb L. Judson, in case you wondered—I'd wrap one around his neck and...well, you get the picture.

The trouble was, the blasted thing kept getting stuck. Every centimeter we gained, a little silver blob would get caught in the zip and something under her clothes would give a little squeak of pain. I could have sympathized with it, having had the experience myself a few times—ouch. We both pulled and jerked until it was freed, and made another centimeter only to be interrupted by another snag and screech of pinched Sploig.

The whole process was not helped by Kik screaming, "Get it off! Get it off!" in my face at the top of her lungs. And let me tell you, she's got some lungs.

I think Kik finally lost patience, if she ever had any.

She grabbed the partially open neck of her jumper and ripped it open from collar to...well, the end of the zipper and then some. My eyes bugged out in shock at what lay beneath. I'd seen Kik *sans* garments about ten thousand times, so that wouldn't have shocked me. What was shocking, and probably just as you guessed by now, the Sploig was having a blanket party with my pilot!

It covered her in a silvery mass from neck to...uh...nether regions. Her hands, face and feet were still Sploig-free, so I tried to get a grip on the slimy mass at the edge. It was kind of like trying to grab a blob of warm, greased bread dough. As soon as I thought I had a grip, it would slip through my fingers and keep spreading. It was edging up her neck now, and Kik was getting a panicked look on her face. Then again, I probably was, too.

"Harry?" she screamed at me, pleading.

Now, Kik has touched more alien flesh than any xenobiologist on record, but I'd never seen her this scared, not even when we were a hair's breadth from being vaporized by a Farfnian patrol cruiser. I guess it hit me a little hard.

I grabbed her hand, just about the only flesh-colored piece of Kik I could get a grip on, and told her, "I've got you, Kik."

I hadn't noticed that we'd stumbled a few steps while we struggled with her jumper, so it was as surprising to me as to Kik when she took one more step back and toppled right into the hole Turk had blasted in the deck.

I don't know if I didn't let go of her hand or if she didn't let go of mine, but the result was the same. I fell forward, sprawling onto the deck like a freshly landed flounder—no name jokes, please. I cracked my chin pretty hard and started muttering show tunes, but that ended abruptly when something jerked my arm so hard I thought it would come off at the shoulder. The force of the jerk cracked my chin against the deck again, silencing the show tunes.

That was when I realized I was up to my shoulder in stringspace and sliding deeper by the second.

Since falling into stringspace was about as attractive a proposition to me as starring in a Carpoolian porn flick, I pulled back. I still had a good hold on Kik's hand, and she was squeezing mine like an agent with a brand-new contract. The problem was, there weren't a lot of things to grab onto, and I was slipping.

I looked around frantically. Yes, frantically. I was frantic, without a doubt. I was so frantic, in fact, that I asked Zook for help. And I didn't even ask nicely.

He was just standing there watching my crew blaze away at the scattering pieces of Sploig, a mildly entertained smile on his lips, evidently unconcerned that his captain was sliding slowly into oblivion. Then again, he'd already done it once, and probably thought it was no big deal. I begged to differ.

"Grab my ankles, you Immortal twit!"

"Oh, right." He moseyed over, or at least it seemed like a mosey from where I lay, and grabbed me by the ankles. "How's that?"

"(expletive deleted) great!" He'd stopped my sliding, anyway. "Now pull!"

"Oh, right."

He pulled, and I actually started to edge out of the pool of nothing that had engulfed me up to the shoulder. Then the whole ship lurched like a drunken sailor, and stringspace evidently decided it had had enough of Kik. It spat her back into the ship like someone finding a bug in their soup. She flew out of the hole in the deck with enough force to be flung free of the Sploig's embrace. That left me lying there with a stringspace-covered Sploig attached to my hand, and Kik just about to finish her abrupt trajectory by landing right on top of me.

Did I mention that we were both screeching in a most undignified manner?

No?

Well, she was, anyway. I was screeching in a very dignified, captain-like manner. Yep...and anyone who tells you different is probably telling you the unvarnished truth. Hey, when my captain's reputation is at stake, I will lie like a rug to preserve it. Ask anyone!

Well, Kik didn't land on me, but only because Turk caught her.

Then Turk fell on me.

After a lot of cursing, crying, screaming, yelling and more cursing, almost all of it mine, we managed to get disentangled. Unfortunately, by the time we managed this, the Sploig had released my hand, the patch of stringspace had oozed away, and neither was anywhere to be seen.

"Damn!" That was me, though I couldn't tell you exactly what I was damning.

"You okay, Harry?" Kik sounded genuinely concerned. I guess it was as good a thank-you as I could expect.

"Marvelous." I managed to get to a sitting position without much help. "Where'd the damn Sploig go?"

"Everywhere," Charley said. He looked so frazzled I thought he might have seen an honest politician or something. "Turk's the only one who bagged a piece. They're too damn fast to shoot."

"Well, at least that's one." I accepted one of Turk's platter-sized hands and made it to my feet, clutching my bruised…uh…parts. Kik's knee had left a permanent dent in a very tender spot. "How many more are there?"

"Just one."

Ice slithered down my spine at the voice.

We all turned to the new figure standing beside the Sploigmobile.

"Don't worry, Harry. The hard part's over. Aren't you glad?" she said, smiling disarmingly.

It was Laila.

"Oh, crap."

CHAPTER NINE

WE'VE BEEN SPLOIGED

"I've gotta say, Harry, you made it difficult," the Laila-Sploig said. "Getting you here was like picking up spilt quicksilver."

"Looks like we've got more in common than we thought, huh, Harry?" Kik's amused tone knocked me out of my stunned silence.

"Huh?" I looked at her, trying to make sense of what she'd said. I was still trying to figure out what exactly was standing in front of me looking like the woman who'd used my heart for a Hacky-Sac®.

"I must admit, I'm a little jealous. You beat me to the Sploig, and from the look of it, you had *four* of 'em!"

Suddenly it all clicked together in my mind with microchip clarity.

I'd been…Sploiged.

I didn't know whether to feel angry, nauseated, or just plain foolish.

"Should I shoot her?" Turk asked in a conversational tone.

"I…uh…" Evidently my brain was at war with my vocal cords again. I don't really remember what I was thinking, or even *if* I was thinking, but in retrospect—always twenty twenty—it's a wonder I didn't tell Turk to vaporize the Laila-Sploig. I mean, what perfect revenge on the clone-turned-alien who broke my heart?

I'd not only been Sploiged, I'd been so Sploiged that I had actually fallen for an alien. Nausea was starting to win out over anger very quickly, and the chicken burritos I had for lunch were in the middle of the argument. Then another thought gelled in my protoplasm-free prosthesis: "But you're not *the* Laila. You're just...just..."

"Well, two of us were part of Laila, and we share experiences, so, well...I guess you could say *we're* Laila."

"I don't believe it!" Denial? You bet your ass, I was in denial! Her voice... Her face... It was *her*. Without a doubt, I'd been deceived from the beginning.

"I think you should let me shoot her, Harry. It'd be good for you. Trust me."

I was beginning to think Turk was right, and who knows, with as many ex-wives as he had, maybe he was speaking from experience.

"Well, I could mix up a batch of margaritas to try and convince you, but it really doesn't matter. Believe me or don't, shoot or don't, stay and find out what we did with Tillamook or go home." She... It? They? Oh, whatever! The Sploig shrugged and smiled that smile that had hooked my heart like a prize bass.

They had us and they knew it, but it didn't make me not want to tell Turk to vaporize my ex-girlfriend.

"Okay, I'll bite. What did you do with Tillamook?"

"Shift the ship into real space and find out."

"What? That'd just take us back to Earth. Kik fell into stringspace, so it would take us back to..." The Laila-Sploig was shaking her head, so I gave up. "Okay, what?"

"One of us was covering her. It read our point of origin from our molecular structure and transported us to our world."

"Whoa," Turk said, his linguini drooping a bit.

"The Sploig home world?" Zook asked, his eyes gleaming like a conservative with a new assault rifle. "Very interesting indeed!"

"But to what time?" I asked. "Is that how you travel in time, using the stringspace thing, but with something from another time?"

"That is paradoxical, Harry. How can you bring something from another time without having a time machine in the first place?" Okay, so Zook was making sense, which really bugged me. But if not using stringspace, then how could we have gotten to the Sploig home world, unless...

"There never *was* any time travel."

"Very *good*, Harry." Laila smiled, and I could have vaporized her myself. Maybe the Sploig wasn't trying to be condescending, but it sure felt like it. Okay, maybe I was being a little sensitive. So what?

"No time travel? Oops. Sorry, Harry." That was Zook, and he was looking a little sheepish, like a kid caught with his hand in the honey pot. "Guess I got a little…uh…overly imaginative."

"But how did they know when to kill Neezl? I mean, he was about ready to tell us everything and *POW*!" Turk trained his weapon back on the Sploig and glared. "What about that, Sploig?"

"It's not *all* about you, Turk," she said with a scoff that almost got her blown into subatomic particles. "You just happened to be there when the robossassins were called in. We'd been deciding for weeks the best time to take them out. Sorry about the firefight, but robossassins don't like to get shot at and tend to shoot back. We certainly didn't mean for any of *you* to get hurt."

"Didn't mean for us to get *hurt*?" Turk's voice was raising an octave every time he spoke. If he didn't shut up, the Sploig would have to change into a dog to hear him.

"Take it easy, Turk," I said, exuding calm. Yes, *exuding*! What's wrong with exuding?

"What do you mean, 'them'?" Kik asked. "Who were they supposed to kill besides Neezl?"

"Oh, sorry." Laila giggled, and I felt my intestines tie into knots. "Neezl and those of us who were Laila were working together before he went native and got himself marked for dismissal." She smiled when we just stared at her. "Neezl was not a Carpoolian, he was Sploig, eight of us, to be precise. We had been watching the Carpoolians for years, which is why Neezl went native."

"Went native?" I had to ask.

"We were what you would call cultural anthropologists."

"Or complete whack-jobs," Charley put in, evidently not buying a bit of it.

Laila ignored the comment.

"We observe other species from inside their culture, but there's always a danger when Sploig stay together in the shape of one sentient species too long. Sometimes they start thinking they are what they look like, and they want to stay that way."

"And Neezl wanted to stay a Carpoolian, so you had him killed."

"Not killed." She made a strange face, rather like she'd just caught a whiff of an unpleasant odor. Maybe she had. Mishi's burritos are pretty spicy.

"We call it 'dismissal' when one or several of us are eliminated from the whole. And that wasn't the only reason they were dismissed. We'd probably have tried to talk them out of it some more, but then he decided to run for president." She shook her head. "They were the ones who tipped off the Farfnians and caused the PPD. They planned the whole thing so they could gain control over Carpool. Sploig could never let that happen. We work strictly behind the scenes. We're invisible, and we like it that way."

"You know, this is all very nice and informative, but it's not answering the question of what the (expletive deleted) you did with Tillamook!"

"Easy, Turk." I put a hand on the muzzle of his linguini and he let me push it out of line with the Sploig. He can get a little tense when people talk over his head, which is pretty much why he's always tense, but I know how to handle him. At least I think I do. When I err, he reminds me, which usually hurts a lot. "Let's let the nice Sploig talk."

"Talk," Turk grunted as if the process of transforming thoughts into words was something to be reviled. Well, for Turk, maybe it was.

"Actually, it would be much easier to *show* you rather than to try to explain." That smile again. Maybe I *would* let Turk vaporize her, just to wipe that smile off.

"And just how do you plan to show us?" Not that I expected her—It? Them? I'm going to go crazy thinking about this!—to tell us the truth.

"I told you. Take the ship back into real space, and I'll show you where we put Tillamook." She shrugged and smiled. "Or shoot me and go home. But I think if you come home empty-handed with a hold full of cheese and no Tillamook, the CEO's going to be a little torqued, don't you think?"

"The CEO's always torqued," I muttered. There was no way around it, I just couldn't let the opportunity to find out the fate of Tillamook slip past. Kind of like walking past a hundred dollar bill lying in the gutter; sure, you can barely make a phone call with it, but you've still got to pick it up. It's an inborn human trait, I think. Or it could just be greed. Yeah. Maybe.

And *maybe* the Turpenoids will win the Lava-Hockey Cup again this year.

You think?

"Zook, you, Turk, Kik and I are going to take Laila and the Sploigettes here to the bridge. I know you don't like weapons, but pick one up anyway."

"Sure, Harry," he said somewhat despondently, taking one of Turk's spares.

"Charley, break out one of the emergency packs and squirt some sealant foam around that thing." I gestured toward the Sploigmobile. "I don't want a leak if we blink back into empty space."

"Oh, don't worry, Harry," Laila said, "we'll be entering real space in an atmosphere."

I gave the Sploig a glare that I usually reserve for parking attendants who have just given me a ticket. "Do it anyway, Charley. And throw a patch over that hole while you're at it." I indicated the hole that Turk had shot in the deck.

"Sure, Harry." Charley shouldered my Cuisinart and gestured for his crew to do as I'd said. Well, at least he didn't argue with me.

"Don't you *trust* me, Harry?"

My glare devolved into the one I reserve for puppy kickers.

"Turk, I have one task for you, and I want you to concentrate on this one task until I tell you differently, okay?"

"Uh, sure, Harry. Name it."

"I want you to point that handful of plasma-powered pasta at this thing and, if it even looks like it's even thinking of changing shape, I want you to blast it into a billion little Sploig fritters, okay?" I was trying for Clint Eastwood, but probably only achieved Bill Clinton on the intimidation meter. Anyway, all Laila did was smile.

"Don't worry, Harry. One false move and she's toast."

Laila raised one eyebrow, looked at Turk, and her smile faded. I hate it when he's more intimidating than me, which is pretty much all the time.

"Let's go then."

I didn't really trust the lift, so we followed one another up the stairs. Aside from Turk having just cut a hole in it, the thought of being trapped in the lift with a homicidal, shape-changing ex-girlfriend was a little unsettling. Not as unsettling as Mishi's Eggplant Surprise, but bad enough to make me wary.

Once we were on the bridge, I felt better. Maybe it was something about confined spaces. I've never been claustrophobic, but I kept having mental images of all the old horror movies I'd seen. Whenever the unsuspecting dork hid in a closet... Ick.

"Kik, if you'd be so kind as to take your clothes off, we'll see what this Sploig has in mind."

"Okay, Harry, but are you sure you want to do this? I mean they could snatch us up as soon as we pop in." Her zipper was already torn from neck to...uh...yeah...there, but Kik looked hesitant.

"That's why I'm going to stay plugged in the whole time, Kik. Anything even looks suspicious, and we pop right back into stringspace. And I don't particularly care if we're too close to something important when we do. Their loss."

"Honestly, Harry. You're so paranoid." The Laila-Sploig was living up to her role as annoying ex-girlfriend. Maybe *she* was going native.

"Being shot at tends to make me paranoid."

"Oh, we weren't shooting at you, Harry. We were shooting to get you where Zook would drop the Limburger on us."

"You *wanted* me to drop the Limburger on you?"

My mouth fell open like the price of air had just gone down. Zook was utterly astounded; I could hear it in his voice. Never in all the years I've known him had anyone caught Zook so completely flatfooted. It was as if the speed of light had just been revoked, the Law of Evolution had just been proven bunk, and a politician had just refused a bribe all at once!

"How else were we going to get aboard?" She laughed at Zook's flabbergasted expression, then at mine. "You two really are something, you know."

That she didn't particularly care about the linguini blaster trained on her, or the fact that Turk was audibly grinding his teeth, bothered me even more than the fact that she'd stumped Zook. I mean, weren't these Sploig scared of anything?

"By the way; how *did* you manage Zook's math question?" Kik asked, looking altogether too sexy in her mutilated jumper to have thought of such a poignant question.

"Yeah, what about the math question?" I refuse to be upstaged by my pilot. Oh yeah, I'm as sharp as any spoon in the drawer.

"That? Oh that's just a simple trick." She made a dismissive motion, as if nothing we had to say made any difference.

"Simple, huh?" I'd had just about enough of being played for the fool, and from the looks on their faces, my crew was with me, for once. "If it's so simple, then show me."

"Oh, Harry, you're such a human."

I wasn't sure, but I thought I'd been insulted.

"Oh, all right then. Go ahead," she said, looking bored and infuriatingly cute at the same time, "say something."

"Say something?" She and I both said in perfect synchrony. "Hey, how'd you do that?" We both said. "Stop it!" Again, together.

"See," she said, "it's just a party trick. Every Sploig picks it up."

"You think you're so smart," Turk growled, flexing his hands on his linguini. Both the situation and my attempts at sexual references toward pasta could have gotten even uglier, but at that moment the Sploig's smile faded and she looked rather lost.

"No, actually, we're not very smart," she said, frowning like a corporate accountant holding a federal subpoena. "It takes four or five of us together to be as smart as just one of you."

"Your intelligence is cumulative?" Zook's eyes widened in something that I thought would have been worry in a sane person.

"Oh, not just our intelligence, our consciousness. For instance, I'm about as sentient as any one of you right now, but," and she paused to whistle a complicated little ditty.

All of the sudden, two of Turk's weapons jumped from their locker, a soiled jumper of mine slithered out of the soiled-jumper hamper, and Kik's foot massager hopped off of the console. All four items grew legs and trundled over to the Sploig, then joined together to form into another Laila.

I would have jumped in surprise or something, but I guess my poor prosthesis had just about run out of RAM.

"See, now there are two of us, each as smart as most humans," they both said in perfect unison, while my imagination had a few really unsavory fantasies. Kik giggled nervously, and I knew we'd been thinking the same thing. Oh, great.

Then the two Lailas did a kind of hug thing, and the before my imagination could take the situation any further down the sewer, we were all staring at a Turk-sized…well…Turk.

"Hey! Stop that!" My security chief seemed less than pleased at the shape they'd chosen, and I had to agree. Watching two copies of my ex-girlfriend change into Turk was going to give me nightmares for weeks. Lucky he didn't blast them and the bridge to bits. Lucky I didn't tell him to.

"Now there are eight of us," they said in Turk's melodious baritone, "and we're easily as smart as Zook."

"Well, thank you, I think," Zook said, stirring from deer-in-the-headlights mode to something resembling cognizance. "So, you've been onboard quite some time, I guess."

"Oh, yes, we've been watching you ever since you picked up Laila on Carpool."

"So you know all about the cheese factory and everything." Turk might be a little slow, but he makes up for it with sheer idiocy.

"That was the whole point, Turk."

"What was?" Turk was right? Now my world was *really* turning on its head!

"Why, cheese, of course." The Turk-Sploig gave us a very readable 'Well duh!' look. "Zook was right about that much. We realized even before Neezl went native that cheese was our ticket back to the top. We just had to figure out how to make the stuff, and we'd have every Farfnian in the galaxy quite literally eating out of our hands."

"So you stole Tillamook." See? I can think ahead, kind of.

"Correct, Harry, we stole Tillamook." She smirked, and I got the feeling she was not telling all. You think?

"So what *did* you do with it?"

"Bring the ship into the real universe, and I'll show you."

"Fine." I nodded to Kik and she shed her jumper with a practiced shrug. Practiced? How about *perfected*. "One word from me, Kik, and we're back in stringspace."

"Before you can blink, Harry." She hopped into the couch and sealed the lid. I plugged in and said "Hello" just to make sure the connection hadn't been Sploiged with.

"Turk, I want you to keep doing exactly what you've been doing, but try not to kill anyone else if you have to vaporize the Sploig, okay?"

"Oh. Okay, Harry." He fiddled with a few noodles, which didn't give me warm fuzzies about what would have happened if the Sploig had made a threatening gesture a few minutes ago.

"Zook, can you manage Turk's console and Engineering?"

"Can a Carpoolian drool?"

"Fine." I strapped on my Jiffy Whip™ and took my seat.

I thumbed the switch for shipwide intercom. "Okay, everyone. We're about to visit the Sploig home world, so if you're not holding a weapon, get one, and if anything sprouts legs and starts to crawl away, aim like you mean it. Fische out."

I took a deep breath and said, "Okay, we're going in, so stay sharp." Damn, I'm macho when I'm scared spitless. I turned on the viewer, gave Kik a mental nod, and held on tight.

The familiar jolt was immediately followed by a blinding blue-white glare that flooded the bridge, eliciting an involuntary gasp of shock that completely blew my previously macho façade. The scene through the viewing screen was so bright I could have used a pair of sunglasses. By the time my eyes adjusted, my brain was already telling me that we weren't in Kansas—or Wisconsin—anymore.

"Holy…" That was Zook, and the shock in his voice was even more worrisome than what my eyes were trying to tell me. I squinted, and tried to take it all in.

"Crap!" That was Turk. At least he was himself—good old Turk—except…

"Turk, watch the Sploig, not the screen!" Okay, I may have been a *little* terse.

I have to admit, I was having a "holy crap" moment of my own, almost literally.

Through the viewing screen I could see a slightly alien landscape curving away from the ship. The problem was, it wasn't curving down like a planet does, it was curving up. I switched the viewer aft, then port and starboard. There were trees and rocks and bushes, but no buildings or structures of any kind. They filled the strangely upward-curving landscape all around us. It was like we were sitting at the bottom of a deep valley, but there were no hills or other topography to obscure the non-existent horizon. That's right, non-existent. There was no sky, just landscape, and it curved up in every direction until it was lost overhead in the glare of a too-bright, blue-white star.

"Dyson Sphere," Zook muttered. "A small one, but a Dyson Sphere."

My prosthesis did a little cross-referencing without my having to tell it to do so, and I got a mental image of what Zook was talking about. A Dyson Sphere is like a planet turned inside out with the landscape on the inside, a diameter roughly that of a planetary orbit, and a star in its middle. But something wasn't right.

"How far across is this thing, Zook?" I asked.

"Sensors can't read straight across. That bloody bright thing is in the way. But with a little math, hmm, about four hundred thousand kilometers, I think."

"Too small," I said. "This isn't a Dyson Sphere. It's a bubble world, and that's not a real star." I looked to our Sploig guide and asked, "Is it?"

"Very good, Harry. You're quicker than we thought." The Turk-Sploig grinned at my glare. "No, it's artificial, just a charged ball of neutronium spinning inside a torus of fusing hydrogen. It'll need recharging again in another hundred thousand years, but it works for now."

"Held in place with a magnetic field, I presume." Well, Zook was sounding more like himself, the twit.

"Yes, actually. One projector at each pole."

I did some math in my head, using Zook's estimates of the proportions that surrounded us. The numbers got very large very fast. The surface area inside would equal that of about a *thousand* Earths. That's a lot of elbow room. "No terracing, so we're not spinning. Artificial gravity, or we'd all be falling into your little neutron sun." See, I'm not *totally* dim.

"You've got it, Harry."

"So where's Tillamook, Sploig?" Turk had taken my rather terse order to heart, it seemed. He looked like he was ready to start a Sploig stir-fry at any moment.

"Let's see, they may have moved it but…" The Sploig stepped over to my chair and smiled down at me. "May we control the viewer for a second, Harry?"

"Uh, sure." Strange, but even though I knew this wasn't Turk standing beside me, I had to keep reminding myself that it wasn't. I don't know why. I mean, it wasn't even really acting like Turk. It punched a few buttons on my armrest and I had to ask the question that had been boggling my brain since I first thought about the Sploig. "What do you really look like, anyway?"

"What?"

There was a little tension there, or I'm no gauge of…well, so this wasn't exactly a *person*, but you know what I mean.

"What do you look like?"

"What do you mean?"

Now it was my turn to look tense, and more than a little confused.

"Well, I was just wondering, you know. Curious, really."

"About what?"

There were major "uh-oh" alarms going off in my head now, but I figured it was too late to back out.

"Your natural state. You know, what do you look like when you're not trying to look like something else?"

"Oh, that. We have no idea." The Turk-Sploig went back to the view screen controls.

Okay, I've never had a problem fitting *both* of my feet into my mouth at the same time, so I said, "How can you not know what you really look like?"

"Why should we care? We take whatever forms please us, or are most functional for the purpose we have in mind." The Sploig finished fiddling with the controls and said. "There. There's Tillamook."

While my mind was boggling anew over a race so obviously advanced that didn't give a flying bat fart about its own origins, or even their original shape, I looked up at the viewer. The tiny un-boggled portion of my overloaded cybernetic brain took the time to analyze what my eyes were telling it, and gave me a reasonably believable answer, considering the circumstances. That is, at that point I would have had no problem accepting the notion of Pinocchio materializing on my bridge, sprouting wings from his ears and playing "God Save the Queen" on a saxophone stuck up his bum, so seeing Tillamook hanging almost upside down about a third of the way around the inside of this gigantic, landscape-coated bubble didn't seem that strange.

Uh-huh…

"Oh, okay. I see it." I squinted at the scene. "Is it just floating there?"

"It's being levitated about a hundred meters off the surface. For everyone's comfort and protection, you know."

No, actually I didn't know, but I didn't think asking why Tillamook would need protection from the Sploig, or vice versa, would be particularly wise at the moment. Yeah, that's me, Mister Wisdom.

"Can we talk to them?" Turk asked. Well, maybe not thinking very much has some advantages; you get the drop on the rest of us in brain overload situations like this.

So, while I was busy doing a quick reboot to clear my head—literally—the Turk-Sploig was telling the real Turk what frequency to use. The next thing I knew, the CEO of Tillamook Cheese was staring goggle-eyed at us through the viewer.

"Who the hell are you?" the bespectacled little man asked. "And who are the Mongo twins?" He gestured to the two Turks and squinted.

"Captain Harry Fische of the *Limburger*, Wisconsin Cheese." That earned me a raised eyebrow. I gestured over my shoulder. "The large man holding the Farfnian blaster is Commander Turk, my security chief. The one who looks like his twin is Sploig."

"What's Sploig?"

That earned *him* a raised eyebrow. "The Sploig are the shape-changers that brought you here. You must be Tom Duprey." I knew him by reputation and the fact that the CEO of Wisconsin Cheese had a dart board with his picture on it hanging in his office.

"Why do you call them that?" Duprey asked, with a nod to signify that I had his name right. "We just call 'em Shifters. They've been workin' with us for a while, and I never heard nobody call 'em Sploig."

"My engineer, Zook here, had heard of them. It's what they were called before they lost power to the Farfnians."

The Turk-Sploig chuckled over my shoulder, and I wondered just how accurate Zook had been on that count. I mean, he was wrong about the time-travel thing, right?

"Whatever. Call 'em swizzle sticks if it makes ya happy." He sniffed and pushed up his thick glasses. "So why are you here, Fische?"

"Actually, they brought us here." I hooked a thumb over my shoulder at the Sploig. "We've been looking for you since you were kidnapped, and—"

"Kidnapped? Who told you we were kidnapped?"

"You weren't kidnapped?"

"We weren't kidnapped."

"I don't think they were kidnapped, Harry."

Smart-ass Immortal.

"Pardon the misunderstanding, but if you weren't kidnapped, how did you get here?"

"We made a *deal*, Captain. I'm sure you can understand that much."

I hate condescension. It makes my eyes scrinch up, which gives me wrinkles, which make me look old and cynical. Well, okay, just old. I tried not to scrinch and said, "Yes, I understand deals, sir. I just didn't think that you would make a deal with the Sp—the Shifters."

"You kiddin'? With their technology and the way they can shape-shift, and our cows and cheese factory, we're gonna make the Carpoolian cheese market look like two kids selling spiked lemonade on a street corner." He leveled a glare at me through his lenses and said, "And you're not invited, Fische, so bug off." The viewer went dead.

"Well, that's gratitude for you! We fly halfway across the galaxy looking for them, and not so much as a thank you." Zook sounded positively hurt, like he'd helped a little old lady cross the street and she'd just whacked him with her cane.

"How do we know that wasn't just another Sploig, Sploig?"

I was actually proud of Turk. His paranoia was inspiring leaps of intellect I'd never thought he possessed.

"Oh, this is just a bit too much!" the Sploig said defensively. "What do we have to do to prove we don't mean to kill you? We could have blasted your ship to bits any time we wanted, and we didn't. We could have disabled your drive in stringspace and left you there. We could have killed you all in your sleep, for cripes sake! You want to go land on their front lawn and talk to them? Go ahead!"

"Okay." I gave Kik a few mental instructions and the *Limburger* lifted above the landscape and made a beeline for Tillamook. "Sorry if we don't appreciate your hospitality, Sploig, but we've been shot at a bit too much to feel chummy with you quite yet."

The Sploig just frowned and crossed his tree-trunk arms as we gained altitude—though that might not be the right term, since we were also nearing the ground above us. This place could get confusing without a real up or down. I know it's really like that on a planet, too, but you can't see the whole surface of the planet at once; looking at people above you standing with their heads hanging down like stalactites is just not natural.

People… I thought. *Wait a second…*

"Uh, one question, Sploig," I said as I moved the viewer around the gently curving landscape. No buildings, no structures, no roads, no huts, not even a Starbucks™. Clearly this place was *not* civilized! "Where are all the other Sploig?"

"You're looking at us, Harry."

Something in the Sploig's voice made me take my eyes from the viewer and look at them. The smug smile matched their half-haughty, half-crazy tone. "What do you mean?"

"Look out the viewer. The landscape, every tree, every bush, every rock is Sploig. The whole interior of this place is Sploig." Its voice had taken on a reverent tone that started my vertebrae clacking together as I shivered. "This is what we are, Harry. Not these small, stupid individuals you see in small groups, but one single consciousness."

I just stared at the screen as we flew toward Tillamook, letting my prosthesis estimate how many Sploig were wrapped up in that much landscape. Once again, the number got very large, very quickly.

"This isn't good, Harry."

I was dumbstruck for a second time that day. I think there was honest fear in Zook's voice.

"Why not?"

"The more there are, the smarter they are." He nodded to the viewer which showed perhaps a few *quadrillion* square *miles* of Sploig. "We're outnumbered in the smarts department, big time."

"Like *that's* something new?" I asked with a chuckle.

I never knew an Immortal could give such a dirty look.

CHAPTER TEN

BUBBLE BUBBLE

Okay, I'm sorry, but I'm just not particularly fond of goats.
I think it's their eyes.

Goats have eyes like frogs. Their pupils are all funky-shaped; I think it gives them good peripheral vision, though I don't know why a goat needs peripheral vision. There are usually so many in a herd that they're facing every conceivable direction, and if one bleats in fear, surely the others will be with-it enough to pick up on the vibe.

Maybe that's the reason for the funky pupils after all. Maybe they're too dim to pick up on the bleating-goat-in-terror vibe.

Not that I usually give a damn about the evolutionary inadequacies of goats, but we were landing the ship on the front lawn of the Tillamook Cheese Factory, and they have a substantial herd of goats. But even if they are too dim for the bleating-goat-in-terror vibe, they sure understood the subsonic thrum of a stringship landing on top of them.

Goats scattered like congressmen from an inquest on political fundraising. I gave Kik a mental suggestion that she try not to squish any of them. It really wouldn't do our situation any good to commit any acts of goat-squishing, even if they do have funky eyeballs.

So, anyway, we landed, squishing no goats.

Kik stepped out of the pilot's couch and into a new jumper in one fluid motion. Yeah…fluid…like milk filling a frosted mug, beads of moisture touching the hazed glass as the creamy liquid plunges and cavorts in waves of ivory white… Huh? Oh, sorry. Anyway, I was trying to check all the readouts on the engineering

118

panel to make sure the engines hadn't overheated, or maybe that all the waste tanks were flushed, or maybe... Okay so I watched her get dressed. What's wrong with that? I need a hobby, don't I?

"You need a hobby, Harry," the Sploig said, breaking my reverie.

Reverie, ogling, what's the difference?

Caught in the act. I hate that.

"And you need to shut the (expletive deleted) up, Sploig," Turk growled. Good Turk. Here's a biscuit.

"Turk, you, Kik and the Sploig are coming with me. Zook, watch the ship."

"Is it going to do something?"

Smart-ass Immortal.

"You know what I mean," I told him. Then I had a thought and whispered a few more instructions into his ear. I was rewarded with a fiendishly approving grin, proof that my alternative plan was thoroughly insane.

Not that I really had a plan, per se. I just wanted to talk to the Tillamookers—Tillamookians?—face to face. I mean, for all I knew they'd done away with all the real Tillamookers and replaced them with Sploig look-alikes.

Me, paranoid? No, surely not.

The problem with paranoia is that you never know if you are being paranoid *enough*.

The four of us left the Limburger by the airlock, since the landing bay still had a Sploigmobile stuck through it. Okay, technically there were eleven of us, but who was counting? Turk kept his eyes and his weapon trained on the Sploig, Kik kept her eyes trained on the main building, and I kept my attention trained on the train.

Yes, Tillamook has a train.

What? You thought I was joking?

The train is a small-gauge rail for tourists who come to visit the cheese factory. Ahh, but I see your confusion at my mention of tourists and cheese. How can a cheese factory have tourists, you ask? Hence the goats.

You see, Tillamook uses the hide-in-plain-sight method of secrecy. They actually do have a functional cheese factory right there for everyone to see, but it's strictly goat cheese, which does as much for the average Farfnian as snorting a few lines of powdered sugar does for the average human. Just for the record, I don't have nearly as much against goat cheese as I do against goats, and I have to admit that it is a marvelously ingenious cover for a cheese factory to be hidden under a cheese factory. Okay, so maybe I'm a little jealous.

Of course, there weren't any tourists now, since we were actually parked on a wedge of dirt floating above the inside of a Sploig-coated bubble, which was, in turn, floating through space. At least I *figured* we were floating through space. We could have been bobbing, dodging, dipping or weaving serpentine through space for all I knew. They should have made this thing with windows. Not having a sky was making it really hard for me to shake the feeling that I was hanging upside down, looking at everything through a fisheye lens.

The little train's whistle went *TOOOT* and broke me out of my fascination with not falling off the grass and into the too-bright artificial sun of the Sploig bubble world. Never was I so happy to hear a train whistle. The little train tooted again, just as it passed underneath the huge fiberglass goat that stood at the entrance to the Tillamook Cheese Factory. The main structure is a lot of shiny metal and glass, with big windows and arches of stainless steel. I guess they were worried about rust when they built it; understandable considering the climate. Of course, there was no climate here. Just noon-bright daylight all the time.

We continued up the walkway, under the goat—did you know it's impossible to walk under a giant fiberglass goat without looking up?—and met a nicely dressed young woman at the front door.

"May I help you?" she asked, giving us a perfect tour-guide smile while cocking her head just so. She was wearing a professionally cut suit and stylish shoes, and her flaxen hair was done up in a tight and rather severe bun. Her nails were manicured and her lips were glossed so highly that the artificial sun was reflecting off of them in a rather distracting glare. The shiny glass doors behind her were closed and, despite her smile, she made no move to open them.

"Yes, as a matter of fact, we'd like to have a chat with Tom Duprey and a few of your stringship crews if you don't mind."

"I'm sorry?" she said, cocking one immaculate eyebrow. "You'd like to speak to who?"

I'll give her credit, she was either very good at playing dumb or her hair color wasn't a dye job. She couldn't actually believe we didn't know the truth about what was under the little goat-cheese factory. Could she?

"I've already spoken with your boss, honey, so the little charade is a bit redundant, don't you think?" Yes, when dealing with women, it is always wise to play the chauvinist. I was losing style points fast, so I gestured to the ship on their lawn and tried to make nice. The goats were nibbling at the flaking paint on the landing struts...oh great. "We're from Wisconsin Cheese. We're just here to talk."

She whipped a tiny little phone out of a tiny little pocket and flipped it open, pressing one button with the tip of a fingernail. The look she gave me while she did this would have peeled more paint off of the *Limburger's* landing struts than a whole herd of goats. Fortunately, I've been dumped by a shape-shifting alien. Nothing affects my delicate sensibilities much anymore.

"*Whom* should I say is calling?" she asked, undoubtedly proud of her diction.

"Captain Harry Fische and the crew of the *Limburger*. And tell him I don't want a piece of his deal, I just want to talk."

"Yes, I *do* remember that last bit. Thank you *so* much."

The sarcasm was getting pretty deep, and Kik didn't have any shoes on, so I gestured us all back a few steps while our ice-princess tour guide muttered quietly into her phone. I thought about calling Zook and having him patch my comm unit into their conversation just to be annoying, but I was doing pretty well in that department already, so I let it slide.

After about three minutes, half of which I'm sure our guide was muttering into a dead phone just to make us wait a little longer, she flipped it closed and smiled sweetly at us.

"This way, please." She waved at the glass doors like a veteran game show hostess, and they swept aside on perfect cue.

"Nice touch," I said, returning her smile with one of my own. Both of us were going to get cavities if we weren't careful.

We dutifully followed our tour guide past a little information kiosk—I don't know where that word comes from, but it's fun to say: kiosk kiosk kiosk. It makes me feel Russian. Oh, sorry, I digress—and she dutifully ignored us. I considered belching just to see if she'd twitch, but thought I'd stick with my bad first impression. The room we were ushered into was only slightly cavernous, with red tile flooring, nice accents of white and stainless steel, and large arched skylight windows. It gave the impression of a functional cheese factory, with full-sized animatronic dioramas of industrious workers milking goats, churning milk into whey, pressing the whey, et-cetera. It was rather like the history lesson I skipped in sixth grade.

I was ignoring it all, just about to the same degree as I had back then, when Kik's nails dug into my forearm. I drew in a breath—No, not to scream. I was just going to tell her to please remove her talons from my flesh—but she stopped me with a wide-eyed look. Something was wrong. Either she had just realized that she'd stepped bare-footed into something unpleasant in our traverse of the goat pasture, or she'd seen something in one of the dioramas that wasn't right. Since she wasn't hopping on one foot and screaming "Eeeewww!", I was tending toward the latter of the two theories.

"Harry, aren't these little scenes just *too* realistic?" she said, squeezing my arm again and shifting her eyes to our right and one of the dioramas. "It's almost like they're alive or something."

"Yeah, almost." I glanced and saw a scene of four workers milking goats, placing the old-fashioned nozzles onto rubber goat nipples over and over again. "Kinda creepy, huh?"

Our guide was ignoring us, a fact of which we both took careful note. We slowed half a step, and Turk and his Sploig look-alike passed.

"Yeah, especially that one." She nodded, and I looked.

I looked at the diorama as we strolled past, and finally saw what she'd picked up. All of the figures were male with rather dark skin and hair, and all wore the same color jumpers, all sweat-stained and mired as if they'd been milking goats all day. But there were four men, and only three goats. One of the goats was being double-teamed, and that's just not right, even in a diorama. I was about to open my mouth and say something when Kik interrupted me again, just in time.

"I wish I'd have brought my *camera*," she said, emphasizing the last word with a squeeze that almost pierced the skin. I looked where we would pass the corner of the diorama, and saw the little panning video pickup.

"Too bad, Kik," I said, knowing for perhaps the first time in my life exactly what to do. As we passed the camera, I flipped one of my cans of Jiffy Whip™ out of its holster, gave it a quick shake, and squirted a dollop onto the lens. A glance over my shoulder as I holstered my multi-functional can of whipped topping revealed a furtive glance above the back of an animatronic goat from one of the double-teaming milkers.

Score one for the cheese-man.

I winked at him and we continued on our way toward a wall sporting a large photograph of men herding goats. I was almost positive that this was our goal, and that the men in the photo were not herding Tillamook goats. It looked like Germany to me, maybe Austria, I don't know. Where do they wear lederhosen?

Anyway, our guide slipped her hand behind the picture and did something that made it slide sideways. Behind it stood two closed elevator doors. She pressed her hand to a small green pad set in the wall, and it lit briefly.

She smiled at us.

We smiled back.

Everyone waited.

The doors went *ding* and opened.

Sheer horror lanced through me at what was revealed when those doors whisked aside. I could not believe my eyes, could not come to grips with what I was seeing. Why, oh, why would they do such a horrendous thing? It made no sense. What purpose could it serve, other than to torture my innermost soul? My stomach flip-flopped, and I swallowed hard, trying to talk it into playing nice.

The elevator was glass.

"Captain Fische," Tom Duprey said with a scowl as he exited the glass-walled horror chamber, "I thought I told you we didn't need your misguided help." The doors closed behind him, and my stomach settled down. At least we weren't going to have to *ride* in the thing.

"You did, but I didn't think that—"

"You didn't think at all, Fische! This is *our* deal with the Shifters, and you're not invited as a partner."

"Now that you mention it, I do remember you saying something like that, but that doesn't mean we can't sit down and talk." I was still trying to be nice, not knowing if I was talking to a Sploig or the real Tom Duprey. I was starting to feel a little like a game-show host: Would the real Tillamookers please step forward? "We just want to make sure you're doing okay, that you've got everything you need. I'm sure the Sploig are quite accommodating, but if you want anything special from Earth, we could bring you a shipment now and then."

"We're fine here, Captain. The Shifters give us everything we ask for. We do miss having a sky occasionally, and we had to install a sprinkler system to keep the grass on the surface green. Never thought I'd miss Oregon's weather." He got a rather wistful look for a moment, and then snapped back to his previously sour mien. "We'll be undercutting your price on the cheese market inside a month. That's why you're here. Admit it!"

"The last thing we want is a deal with the Sploig," I assured him quite honestly. I didn't like being manipulated, and having dated a Sploig for some time—shudder—I was going to make damn sure it wasn't happening to the Tillamookers without their knowledge. Tom seemed real enough, right down to his rudeness, but if I could be fooled by Laila on a much more intimate level—

double shudder—I'm sure a Sploig could play a convincing Tom Duprey. "They've been running us around half the galaxy, evidently as eager to get us here as we were to find you. I'd like to know why before I leave."

"*They* brought you here?" His eyebrows joined in the middle of his forehead into one long, furry caterpillar as he scowled at the Turk-Sploig. "I don't believe it! You're here to horn in on our deal."

"Actually, Tom, we *did* bring them here."

Duprey's face fell like a bridegroom's trousers. Unless they were really playing us for some reason, this was the real Tom. Our tour guide, however, just stood there with a vacant look on her face. *Sploig*, I thought, *or a natural blond*.

"*You* brought them here? Why?"

"Because we hadn't counted on Captain Fische discovering the secret of traveling through stringspace without using strings."

"*He* discovered it?" Duprey looked at me like I'd grown an extra brain on the top of my head. It's *so* nice to have a reputation.

"Well, I can't take all the credit, but yes, we figured out the basics on our own, thank you."

"By accident," the Sploig added.

"Serendipity," I countered, "while saving *your* ass from a nuclear missile, if you remember."

"Actually, the portion of us that was part of Laila is currently not our ass, but more over here." The Turk-Sploig pointed to its upper left thorax. "And if you think we're going to thank you for that, you're sorely mistaken, Captain. The continuation of a few individual portions of the whole of us is inconsequential. What matters is that you have discovered a secret that we did not intend you to discover. That is why we brought you here."

"I don't get it," Kik interrupted, proving once again that she's not just a stunningly beautiful woman with a striking figure, sharp wit, and acerbic temper, as well as an awesome pilot.

Okay, so maybe I've got a deeply repressed *thing* for her. I'll admit it, but it would never work out. I'm human, remember?

"If we found something out you didn't want us to, why not just kill us?"

All of that and a big mouth, too.

"Three reasons, Kik," The Sploig said with a smile that was so not-Turk that it set all the hairs standing up on my neck. "First, we needed to inform the rest of us what you had discovered. Second, we had to keep you from divulging it to the rest of humanity."

I remembered several conversations I'd had with Laila, usually late at night when my brain was addled and recovering from extensive…software testing…if you get my drift. Invariably, she had gently argued against filling in the rest of Wisconsin Cheese about the specifics of our discovery of traveling without strings. Oh, there had been a lot of loose talk, especially during our rather tumultuous homecoming, but we'd never brought up the possibility of using the technique on a large scale. Sometimes I'm astounded by my own stupidity. I could see where this was going, and didn't like it. The light at the end of the tunnel was very likely a train.

"And now that we're here, and your secret is safe?" Turk asked, fidgeting with his linguini blaster. I could see that his paranoia was still substituting nicely for intelligence. He saw the same light I was seeing, and maybe even heard the train whistle.

"Which brings us to the third reason we didn't kill you." The Turk-Sploig smiled again. I wished it would stop doing that. It made me nervous. Worse yet, it made Turk nervous. "We want to offer you a deal."

"I *knew* it! You back-stabbing, two-timing, double-dealing…" Tom's face was turning a familiar shade, which made me wonder if turning mauve was a trait that all cheese-company CEO's had in common.

"Calm down, Tom. We will keep our deal with you, but you must understand, if we don't bring Harry and his crew into our little family, they will tell all the rest of Wisconsin Cheese about the secret, and that will threaten our plans. They will be able to deliver cheese anywhere in the galaxy as fast and as secretly as we can. That, we cannot allow."

"And if we don't deal, you kill us." I could have slapped Turk, but he was just nervous enough to vaporize me for it.

"We won't kill you, Turk," it said, and it sounded especially strange, since it was using Turk's voice to say it, "but we won't allow you to leave here."

I always hated that part.

The other part I hated was that I'd completely forgotten about our clandestine goat milker. Everyone was so intent on each other that he had managed to sneak up on the tiny troupe unnoticed. Now he stood behind our former tour guide.

"Dey lie!" he snapped, one hand snatching her by the hair while the other brandished a wicked little knife. "Dey do not kill ju, dey replace ju! Dey take ju and come back to Earth and replace *everyone*!"

He was quite hysterical, and his deep accent was hard to grasp. It didn't sound Oregonian. But what was even harder to grasp was the calm on our tour guide's face.

"Who the hell are you?" Tom asked incredulously, aghast at the sight of the knife.

"I am Jorge. I work for ju. I milk de goats."

"You milk the goats?" Tom asked, eyebrows arching quizzically. Obviously, this was all news to him.

"I jused to milk de goats. Now dere are no goats. I hide. I watch."

"There are no goats?" Tom was getting good at asking baffled questions. He should have made a career of it. He wasn't doing too good at anything else right now, such as grasping reality. He was in for quite a shock.

"No. No goats. Only dese tings." He indicated the woman he held by putting his knife at her throat. She didn't react. "Dey took the goats. Dey took the lady who was de tour guide. Dey took many people. Dey will take us all!"

I remembered the goats nibbling at the peeling paint on the landing struts, and had a bad thought. I suppressed the desire to call Zook and tell him the bad news; he'd find out soon enough.

"Calm down, Jorge," the Turk-Sploig said, utterly calm and unworried. Of course, I had no real way to tell if it was worried or not, since I was using its human mannerisms as clues. "We haven't replaced anyone. Least of all, your goats."

"Oh jes ju have! I can tell de difference! I know how to tell de difference. Dis is how ju tell de difference between de real and de Shifters!" He grabbed our tour guide by the wrist and slashed his knife across the back of her hand.

Tom and Turk gasped, but Kik and I had already figured it out. The wound gaped, showed silvery for a second, then closed. He let go of her and backed away, still brandishing the useless knife.

"Ju see? It is not human. De girl, she is gone."

"Gone?" Tom looked at the two Sploig, horrified. "Where did she go?"

"That is unimportant, Tom," the Sploig said with a dismissive shrug. "She and the others were replaced because they did not want to be part of our deal."

"Unimportant? What do you mean, unimportant?" He was obviously having difficulty grasping all of this. It was becoming crystal clear to me. The Sploig had just been caught in an outright lie, and still they were trying to talk their way out of it. Obviously, nothing they said could be believed, which started me wondering about a lot of stuff they'd said aboard the *Limburger*.

"These individuals could not be allowed to stand in the way of our deal. This is how we will gain control over the Farfnians. This is how we will regain our place. Those who were cooperative are here, those who were not have been replaced."

"How could you?" Tom asked, still not getting it.

"They don't think the same about people as we do, Tom," I said, making a motion that told Turk and Kik to back away from the Sploig. "I think you're going to have to renegotiate your deal."

"How many?" Tom asked, glaring at the Sploig. He was backing away, too. "How many of my people have you killed?"

"I...don't know." The Turk-Sploig looked at the Tour-guide-Sploig and the two joined hands briefly. Their hands melded together and they both nodded. "Sixty two, if you count the goats."

Everyone looked at Jorge.

"Ju had forty goats, Señor," he said, shaking his head sadly, though whether for his goats or the dead Tillamookers, I couldn't tell.

"Twenty-two people…" Tom's face was a little strange, his eyes were wide, but it didn't look like he was seeing anything. I knew how he felt, but when it happened to me, it was usually a software glitch. Then he focused on the Sploig and said, "Our deal is over. Take us back to Earth."

"We can't do that, Tom, and you know it. The Farfnians know something is going on, and if we take you back, they could learn of us. We can't allow that."

"Can't allow?" Tom turned that color again, and I knew he was going to do something stupid. "I'll show you what you can't allow!" He pulled a small control pad out of his jumper pocket and flipped open a covered switch.

Now, I'm not one to tell someone when to or when not to do something stupid, but when I'd already made plans to be stupid, and I couldn't have him upstaging me.

"Hang on there, Tom. Don't do anything drastic." *Like blow us all to smithereens*, I thought. What exactly is a smithereen, by the way? I've always wondered. "We can help you out."

"Can you fit seventy people and two hundred cows in your ship, Fische?"

"Uh…no, but—"

"Well, I guess we could load our ten ships, too, but—"

"You will not be taking your cows, Tom."

"Oh, we won't?" He held up the controller, his thumb on the switch.

"Tom. Please. We can get everyone back to Earth, but they're right about one thing, when we get back, the crabs are going to be all over you like…well, like crabs."

"I thought you said you couldn't fit everyone in your ship."

"I can't."

"Well, I can't fit all our cows in our ships either, so how are you going to get everyone back?" Tom was looking a little strained, so I figured I'd just show him. The trick was to do it without the Sploig having an opportunity to kill everyone.

"Just tell your people to hang on, Tom." As he did so, I clicked open my own comm unit and said, "Zook?"

"Yes, Harry."

129

"Are you ready?"

"Yes, Harry."

"Will it work?"

"If it doesn't, it should be very interesting."

Interesting. Great. Well, if you're going to do something stupid, there's no point in being indecisive as well.

"Do it."

"Yes, Harry."

I clicked the comm unit closed and smiled to my crew. "Hang on."

They did.

"Just what are you planning on—"

The Sploig was interrupted by that peculiar little jolt of stringspace shift. Sudden and utter darkness filled all the building's windows.

"We're taking Tillamook back to Tillamook," I said, grabbing a railing just before a horrendous jerk broke my grip and sent me flying to the floor. My head hit something, but I was lucky and didn't break into song. When my eyes cleared and my ears stopped ringing, I felt another soft jolt, and bright yellow light streamed through the windows.

Well, it wasn't *that* bright. We *were* in Oregon, after all. It was raining.

CHAPTER ELEVEN

TRAINS, GOATS AND CHICKEN LITTLE

As I got to my feet I noticed that Turk was the only one who hadn't been knocked flat by the jolt. The railing he'd grabbed to steady himself was bent, but he was still standing. He was also the only one holding a gun, which gave me a perverse sense of security. Being back on Earth helped in that department, too. Nothing like a rainy, overcast sky and real green hills outside the windows to make you feel at home.

"What the hell just happened?" Tom squawked, vaulting to his feet and rubbing a sore spot on his impressive backside. "Where the hell are we?"

"Tillamook." I dusted myself off while Tom started to grin slowly and the two Sploig—although there were really closer to a dozen—looked at each other in expressionless silence.

"Your species does not have the technology to do this," our tour guide said, looking at me, then back to her Sploig partner.

"His engineer is an Immortal," the Turk-Sploig said with a continental drift-like shrug. "It is quite resourceful."

"Turk, keep a close eye on our—" But before I could finish, both Sploig fell apart and scattered in twelve different directions.

Turk shouted a warning and fired twice, creating two small craters and decreasing the number of Sploig by a sixth before they skittered, slithered, flapped, and flopped out of sight.

"We've got problems," I said to Tom. "I have no idea how many of those things there are around here, but I'd guess quite a few."

"We'll round 'em all up." He stepped over to Jorge and clapped him on the shoulder. "Hor-hey here knows how to spot 'em."

"It's Jorge," he said, standing a little straighter and eyeing his boss rather warily. "Are we really on Earth? And does dis mean I get a promotion?"

"We're on Earth, all right," I said.

"And you can be my personal security man, if that makes you feel better. Now, how do we get rid of these pesky things?" Tom brushed his hand on his pants surreptitiously, but kept smiling at Jorge. I can't say as I blamed him; Jorge had a distinct aura of goat about him that was rather pungent.

"De shifters, dey do not bleed." Jorge made a quick motion with his knife. "You stick everyone; de ones who bleed are human. De ones who don't bleed, you shoot."

"You're going to have to stick all the cows, furniture, clothing and everything else, then," Kik explained. "They can look like anything. I've been massaging my feet with one for…well, I don't know how long."

Lucky Sploig, I thought, glancing down at her bare toes.

"Well, maybe we could fumigate the place or something."

I was going to offer a more intelligent suggestion—no, really—when my comm unit bleeped and Zook's elated voice said, "Harry, things just got *very* interesting."

"That means we've got bigger problems," I explained to Tom as I took the call. "What's wrong, Zook?"

"Well, aside from the minor inconvenience of being attacked by a herd of shape-shifting goats, the Farfnians have decided to finish the task that the Sploig started."

"Crap!" I said emphatically, trying to maintain my captain-ness. My perfect rescue of Tillamook was about to get squashed.

"Does he mean…?" Tom's question faded as he looked up, as if his gaze could penetrate the ceiling and clouds to discern if the sky was falling.

"He means Chicken Little was a prophet," I said with no small amount of sarcasm. "Sorry, Tom, but I think you're out of the frying pan and in the fire."

"Goats?" Jorge asked, then frowned. "There are no goats!"

"You think?" Kik asked, nudging Turk. "You got a couple extras?" She nodded to Tom and Jorge.

"Always," he said, producing two business-like guns from his jumper and handing one to each of the men. Kik still had her laser pistols.

"Zook, how long do we have?" I asked, checking my own arsenal and finding my two cans of whipped topping ready to squirt. It was refreshing that Turk hadn't offered me a gun. I think he'd finally gotten it through his tiny little cerebellum that I was more dangerous to the good guys than the bad guys with a gun in my hand.

"We have all eternity, Harry. Time is a ceaseless medium, the only constant in the universe, though it can be perturbed by gravitational flux and the occasional—"

"I *meant*, how long do we have until the meteor hits!" I was in no mood for his cockeyed comments, and there was a certain amount of hysteria in my voice that must have gotten the point across. If not the hysteria, the fear, terror, horror, anxiety and desire to scream for my mommy that were also vying for supremacy of my voice may have helped add a touch of urgency.

"Oh, sorry. Twelve minutes forty-six seconds."

"Time to go," I told Tom as his eyes widened to the point that I thought his eyelids would flip over his forehead. "Tell your people."

"Go how? Even if we could get everyone aboard and fly them out, not to mention the cows, they'll just shoot us down."

"The Sploig didn't tell you how to navigate stringspace without strings?"

"No. They told us they could take us wherever we wanted, anywhere in the galaxy, but not how."

"Nice." I quickly filled him in on the technical details of the process. It took about thirty seconds, and I was amazed that his eyes could indeed get wider. "So, get on the comm and tell your captains. Cram as many cows as you can into the holds of your ships. Check them all to make sure you're not bringing on Sploig.

Guns would be a good thing. I'll have Zook transmit the codes to get you into WCC. You can hole up there until things cool off."

"Uh, okay." He opened his comm and broke the bad news to his people, including the part about the murderous shape-changing aliens in their midst. They took it pretty well. At least, I didn't hear any screaming, but we were several floors above the facility, so the hysteria may have been somewhat muffled.

"Not that I don't appreciate your hospitality, Tom, but my crew and I need to get to the *Limburger*." I checked my watch. "We've got about ten minutes until this place is a crater."

"I will stay with Señor Tom," Jorge said emphatically, brandishing his new sidearm. I couldn't have been happier, considering his distinct eau de goat and his willful disregard as to where the business end of his weapon was pointed. I don't think he knew it would take out a wall.

"Good. You be careful."

Turk, Kik and I turned to go do battle with the goats when the lift doors opened. Someone shrieked, someone swore and then someone else fired a weapon. We turned back to see Jorge pointing his pistol at the lift doors, and a terrified-looking little fellow standing there with his hair smoking where Jorge had singed it with a blast that had taken out a good portion of the back of the glass elevator. I smiled. The poor fellow looked like he was about ready to evaporate from fright, but Tom waved us on.

"Don't worry, I'll check him. Go!"

While Tom brandished Jorge's knife and advanced on the terrified little man, I grabbed my pilot and headed for the door. I checked my watch again—nine minutes now, definitely time to fly. But even that wasn't as easy as I'd hoped it would be. Through the glass doors we could see several very ugly things running around outside. Laser and small arms fire chased them around the field. I hoped it was coming from the *Limburger*, not some gun-toting Sploig.

Turk was leading the way. I guess he was in a hurry.

The shot from his linguini blaster took out most of the front of the building and vaporized all four legs of the larger-than-life goat. It landed with an unbelievable crash and a cloud of shattered fiberglass. There was now a huge cracked goat butt blocking the entrance, its stiff three-foot tail sagging pitifully on shards of splintered plastic. There was far more wreckage in our way now than there would have been if Turk had simply opened the door, but I wasn't about to find fault with his methods. He was in kill-it-if-it-moves mode, and I wasn't too sure he would be able to tell the difference between me and a goat-impersonating Sploig.

"This way!" he shouted, turning right and sprinting away. Since arguing was out of the question, we followed him.

The rain was a bit of a surprise. Wet and cold, though not hard, it was enough to plaster my hair flat in a few yards, and had me squinting at the dashing shapes and wiping at my eyes. We had skirted the edge of the fallen fiberglass goat when Kik screamed and fired wildly right past my ear.

I figured ducking would be a good strategy, whether to avoid her fire or whatever she was firing at, so I fell flat on my face in the grass. Strategy…yeah. Kik yelped, and I remembered that I was still holding onto her arm. I'd pulled her down with me. Call it strategically planned clumsiness.

"Sorry!" I yelled, trying to right us both. Then I saw what she'd been shooting at, and my poor prosthetic brain tried to jump out of my head and run away in terror. "What the hell?"

I've been on more alien worlds than the Galactic Census Bureau, and I've never seen anything like the thing that was stalking toward us. It looked like a goat that had been crossed with a rabid hyena, then had all of its legs bent sideways with one extra joint added. Throw in huge fangs and long clawed hands, and paint it like someone's bad wallpaper, and you've got a fair picture. It had leapt off of the pile of wreckage and missed us, either due to its own bad aim, Kik's good aim, or my lack of coordination. Whatever the cause, I was glad that it hadn't landed on us.

"Shut up and run!" Kik screamed, firing again as I pulled her up. She burned a hole right through its head. It didn't seem to notice.

"Uh-oh," she said, taking careful aim and firing again. Another hole, right through its chest. It hissed and started forward.

"We're in trouble, Harry."

"Yep." I couldn't think of anything intelligent to say, and I've always lived by the axiom that if you can't think of anything intelligent to say to a woman, just agree.

Hey, it works!

We stumbled backward, unable to tear our eyes away as it moved toward us like a sick parody of a stalking predator. Kik fired several more times, but the narrow beams just burned little holes that closed right up. Then my heel hit something and I fell backward, dragging Kik down for a second time.

She yelped, something hard hit my backside, and I yelped. Her yelp was an octave higher than mine, which saved some of my pride, but her landing on top of me bruised something else that is almost as dear to me. I pushed her off and we scrabbled backward.

Then it leapt.

I really wasn't expecting the train whistle, so even in my horror-stricken fascination with this beast leaping at me for the kill, I had to look.

Good thing.

I grabbed Kik and rolled. Maybe she thought I was being gallant, saving her from the pouncing beast, but she didn't complain.

I caught a glimpse of the goat-Sploig landing a fraction of a second before the little train smashed into it, then into the wrecked fiberglass goat. We both gaped in astonishment as the little engine exploded in a burst of steam and fire, incinerating the Sploig and starting a nice blaze amid the fragments of fallen fiberglass ungulate.

I could learn to like trains.

"Would you two stop screwing around!" Turk bellowed, stepping back around the remnants of a shattered fiberglass teat and glaring at us. "We're a little pressed for time!" He paused to fire at a pouncing goat thing and grinned. Sploig might be able to stand up against a laser pistol, but a Farfnian linguini blaster turned them into little Sploigettes—ick—that spattered the ground in a shower of silvery ooze.

I checked my watch. Seven minutes.

Well, time flies when you're having fun, I guess.

Kik and I looked at each other, our noses about half an inch apart, and I'll be damned if we didn't both blush. Why is it that whenever something tries to kill us, I wind up lying with this xenophile in my arms? Coincidence? Well, if not, I could learn to like having things try to kill me.

We both muttered unintelligible things that neither of us would remember, disentangled ourselves, and lurched to our feet. A railroad rail had made a significant dent in my butt, and walking hurt, but at that point I was prepared to run barefoot over broken glass to get to the *Limburger*.

We ran for our lives.

Charley, the security crew, and the rest of the cargo handlers were fanned out around the airlock ladder, firing at anything that looked Sploig-like. I was hoping that didn't include us. It looked like the Sploig were trying to climb up the landing gear or jump and scrabble up the side of the Sploigmobile that still hung from the ship's underside like a dented limpet. They were trying to get aboard, but my crew are all slightly better with weapons than I am—okay, a lot better—and they were denying the aliens access. Good crew...

"Get aboard!" I yelled as we dashed up. I pushed Kik up the ladder, and not for the reason you're thinking, you sicko. I needed her to pilot the *Limburger*, and the longer she stayed outside, the bigger the chance something vaguely goat-like would pounce on her.

"Go!" Turk yelled in my ear, firing at something that leapt up over the ring of crewmen. It exploded and spattered us with silvery tapioca, or something about that consistency.

I went.

I looked back from the airlock and was gratified to see the rest of the crew falling back and climbing up after me. Turk was quickly draining the power cell of his weapon and making a sizable dent in the Sploig population; he didn't miss a lot. I guess that elevator didn't do so much damage after all.

Inside, I dashed to the bridge, puffing up the stairs after Kik, and thanking my lucky stars that I was male. Okay, so I watched;

what's the harm in watching? It's not like I was thinking impure thoughts or anything. Well, okay, define "impure". Maybe I *do* need a hobby.

Anyway, when we got to the bridge she was already halfway out of her jumper, so I averted my eyes, or tried to, at least, and got to work. Zook was at Turk's console, so I took communications and called Tom while I glanced at my watch. His haggard face materialized on the viewer.

"Five minutes, Tom. How you doing?"

"A little busy!" There was a scream from someone just offscreen, and a hail of fire. He cringed and wiped a gob of silvery goo from his cheek. "These things are coming out of the (expletive deleted) woodwork!"

"Looks like you've figured out how to spot them."

"Yeah," he said, nodding to a tall dark-haired woman who stepped into the picture. "Brite, my engineer, rigged up a microwave emitter that smokes them out, though it tends to catch things on fire."

"Smart!" I said, sparing a smirk for Zook.

"I cannot think of *everything*, Harry," he said in a rather hurt tone.

"Well, that's news to me. You should be gone in about four minutes, Tom. Are your crews about ready to pop out of here?"

"Some are already gone." He nodded to someone who was giving him data from offscreen. "We've got a fix on the asteroid. We'll be gone by the time it hits, but we're going to have to leave some of the herd behind." He sounded like he was about ready to cry. "Damn waste, but there's no way around it. They just won't fit."

"Sorry, Tom." I plugged my brain into the ship's computer and asked Kik if she was ready.

"Any time, Harry, but you may want to check to make sure everyone's aboard. Turk gets a little distracted when there's stuff to shoot."

"Right. I don't want to blink out until it's close anyway," I told her, then said to Tom, "Take off when you're ready. We're going to hang on until the last second. Make it look like they took us out."

"Smart. Careful, Fische. Oh, and thanks. We were all as good as dead with those damn things."

"Buy me a drink some time," I said, clicking off the viewer. I clicked open the shipwide intercom and gave the crew a time update. "Everyone needs to be onboard in two minutes! No exceptions! We're going to blink into stringspace without taking off, so there won't be a warning."

I switched on the external viewer. I couldn't see the airlock, but I could see flashes of weapons fire, and the occasional blinding blast of Turk's blaster. I figured he'd be the last aboard.

I switched the viewer to another angle and noticed that the sky was getting brighter. Chicken Little was right after all. I started giving Kik a countdown, using my link with the computer to time it right. I figured five seconds would give us plenty of room for error.

Either I was getting braver or dumber with my experiences. Maybe both.

I had about forty-five seconds, so I gave the crew an update, telling them, "Everyone aboard right now! We are leaving!"

I glanced at the viewer again. The firing had stopped, and the only reason Turk would have stopped shooting Sploig was if they were locked out and he was locked in. On top of that, the sky was getting very bright. I thought it would be interesting to turn the viewer skyward and tell Kik to shift us into stringspace when I saw the meteor punch through the cloud cover, but considering the thing was probably falling at several thousand miles per hour, that didn't leave much room for error.

Then I realized that I was starting to think like Zook, and that was scarier than any meteor in the universe!

I checked the chronometer in my head and gave Kik a count from five. She shifted us out of real space right on the mark, and the viewer went dark.

"Well, that wasn't so bad now, was it?"

"No, Harry," Zook said with a stifled yawn. "Not bad."

Then the intercom bleeped.

"Fische here," I said, thinking that we probably had stowaway Sploig to deal with.

"Harry, it's Charley. You better hang on."

"Why, what's wrong?"

"It's Turk. He's outside."

"Oh, cr—" A horrendous jolt flung me across the bridge, and my head hit something hard.

And then there was singing…

CHAPTER TWELVE

TURK OVERBOARD

After a few sharp blows to the temple from Zook, I stopped singing *Candyman* and got to my feet. By the time I came back to my senses, Kik was already dressed—damn it—and everyone was looking at me for direction. I managed to get to my seat and thumb open the shipwide intercom.

"All hands!" I wonder about that phrase sometimes. Why not "All feet?" I don't wonder much, mind you, but I wonder. "All hands, this is a Code Gouda! I repeat, Code Gouda! Man overboard!"

I had no idea what that would accomplish, since we weren't even in real space, couldn't launch lifeboats, throw floating objects, or try to recover our lost comrade by venturing out into the...well...stringspace stuff that surrounded us. Scanners and visual pickups were blank, and anyone who went out would have to feel his way around to find anything.

Even something as big as Turk could get lost pretty easily in that stuff.

Maybe the sharp blows to the temple had knocked something loose, but I'd be damned if I'd let Turk remain lost. He was lost enough when he was onboard.

"Zook, grab whatever you think we might need and meet us at the airlock." I had no idea what we'd need, so I was really hoping he'd come up with some good ideas. "Kik, come on!"

"But Harry, if the ship shifted, won't he just get thrown back into the airlock, like Zook?"

Kik had a point. Several, actually, but I will refrain from discussing her finer points right now. I looked to Zook and asked, "Well?"

"I don't think so, Harry." Zook shrugged and cocked an eyebrow in mild amusement. "If he maintained contact with the ship during the transfer, he may still be with us. I don't remember feeling the shift when I was outside in stringspace, but I traveled with the ship."

"That's good."

"But I'd just gone out of the airlock, so it threw me right back in. Turk was outside the whole time. There were a lot of Sploig out there, too. We could have been shifted right back to the Sploig bubble world."

"That's not so good."

"Then again, he could have been—"

"Tell you what, Zook," I interrupted, knowing he could go on like this forever, "why don't we just go find out?"

"Oh. Okay, Harry." He sounded positively cheerful. The twit.

Zook headed off for Engineering to get what he needed, and Kik and I headed for the airlock. The trundling trip down the stairs to the main deck was uneventful, or would have been if Kik had been wearing anything under her jumper.

Note to self: Get a hobby. Or a girlfriend.

When we got to the airlock, Charley, three of Turk's security men, and a few of the other cargo handlers were busily standing in a semicircle around the open outer hatch, biting their fingernails and muttering indecisively. It seemed like a good approach to the problem, and I was just about ready to take up the practice myself when they all looked at me like I was supposed to suggest a better course of action.

"He was at the bottom of the boarding ladder when we shifted into stringspace," Charley informed me, as if this tidbit would help in my analysis of the situation. It didn't.

"And he wasn't aboard the ship, why?" I asked, more to shift the subject away from me deciding what to do next than anything else.

"Well, he was a little busy." Charley made a few gestures with the weapon he'd been using to help decrease the Sploig population. "His gun had run out of juice, and he was trying to fight two or three of the things off and climb the ladder without dropping it. I was trying to help him, but I'm not that good a shot, and I was afraid I'd hit him instead of the Sploig."

"So Turk was fighting two or three Sploig hand-to-hand, trying to climb the boarding ladder, and didn't want to drop his linguini blaster." They all nodded. "Sounds like Turk."

I started biting my nails and staring at the black nothingness that filled the airlock door.

"You gonna *do* something, Harry, or just stare at the door?"

I gave Kik an irritated look for suggesting that I *wasn't* doing something—chewing your fingernails is a time-honored activity—and said, "Well, at least he had a hold on the ship. Maybe he's still with us. Anybody got a rope?"

"Yeah! Here!" One of the cargo handlers fished a coil of light line from a satchel slung over his shoulder and thrust it into my hands.

I could have smacked him.

Now I was going to be expected to *do* something with the rope, and chewing my fingernails had already gotten bad reviews. The captainly, heroic thing to do, of course, was to tie the rope around my waist and dive into the swirling pit of blackness to save my comrade. Since I wasn't feeling particularly captainly or heroic, I snapped my fingers in exasperation and said, "Damn! If I only had a spacesuit!"

One of the security guards cracked open an emergency supply cabinet that I didn't even know was in the airlock, and handed over a slightly dented but quite functional spacesuit. It even had little clip things all around the waist, evidently for the ready attachment of rope so the unfortunate wearer of the suit is not lost beyond hope of retrieval during extravehicular activities.

Great.

I was starting to look around for something else I needed that wasn't readily available when I found myself being helped into the aforementioned spacesuit and commended on my captainly decisiveness and heroic action. By the time I was ready, going for a walk outside wasn't looking quite so bad; the crap was getting pretty deep in here, so any way out was starting to look attractive.

I was just about ready to step through the door when Zook arrived with an armful of equipment and started pouting that I got to have all the fun. Where the hell was he five minutes ago when I really needed someone stupid to volunteer for this? I told him his timing sucked, and started to exit the airlock.

"Uh, Harry?" I turned at the grip on my forearm, and Kik's stare caught me a little off guard. It's hard to tell when she's worried, since she's got no eyebrows to arch, but I've gotten pretty good at reading her face. Yes, I *do* look at her face occasionally, and she *was* worried.

"Yes, Kik?" Something did a little flip-flop in my stomach, either lunch or something more visceral. I hoped it was the latter, since a spacesuit is not only a very unpleasant place in which to hurl, but also incredibly expensive to dry-clean.

"You might want to close the face plate." She reached up and flipped the clear face shield closed, smiling a little crookedly and shaking her head. She said something else, but I couldn't hear her through the closed helmet. It's probably a good thing I'm not very good at reading lips; what I thought she said would have really spoiled the moment.

I said, "Thanks," then remembered that she couldn't hear me either.

I stepped outside.

Two things surprised me: First, it was a lot darker than I thought it would be. Second, there was no gravity. If I'd been thinking rationally I'd have known both of these things would happen, but this was no time to start thinking rationally. Rational people don't step out of perfectly good spaceships when they are in stringspace. Besides, thinking irrationally had always worked well for me, and I wasn't likely to change now.

I worked my way down the ladder by feel, which was hard in the suit. I started wondering how long it had been since we shifted into stringspace. Unfortunately, my brain has a built-in chronometer, and I didn't like the answer it came up with. Turk had been outside for almost eight minutes. That's a long time to hold your breath. I would have started worrying about brain damage except for two things: First, I wasn't expecting to find him at all in this pitch-black soup, and second, this was Turk we were talking about. He didn't have that much to damage.

I know, I'm not one to talk. My own brain is deader than yesterday's pot-roast.

Anyway, since fumbling around in the dark has always been one of my specialties—having done it most of my life, albeit figuratively—I must have gotten pretty good at it by now. Either that or I got lucky.

Whichever it was, when my foot encountered something on the next rung of the ladder, and when that something reached up and grabbed my ankle tight enough to stress the bones to the breaking point, my level of astonishment could only be measured by what it would cost to clean the inside of my spacesuit.

I was recovering my wits—and control over my bodily functions—and thanking my lucky star that my crew couldn't hear what had passed my lips in that singular moment of terror, when a voice crackled in my ear. Maybe I should have picked a different star.

"You all right, Harry?" It was Zook.

Great.

"Fine, why?" Calm…yeah…I was calm…

"I patched your suit intercom into the shipwide circuit," he said, confirming that my ego could indeed take another beating. "We heard something like a baby crying."

"Must be some interference," I explained in as adult a tone as I could manage.

I reached down to whatever had hold of my ankle. I felt a wrist and grabbed it. The grip on my ankle slacked and I pulled. The next thing I knew something very strong had hold of me around the waist. I managed to control my outburst this time, both vocal and…uh…other than vocal. I felt around blindly and confirmed that whatever had hold of me was Turk-shaped.

"I think I found Turk, but I can't climb up and hold onto him at the same time. Pull me up!"

"Right. Hang on!"

"Hang on to what?"

"Uh, sorry about that, Harry. Just let go of the ladder. We'll pull you up."

"Right." I waited until I felt the line pull hard on us before I let go, or tried to. My fingers were obeying commands about as well as my crew, so it took a little convincing to release my grip on the ladder. The grip around my waist was spasmodic, first hysterically strong, then weak, and I didn't want to lose my cargo, so I grabbed hold of Turk. At least I fervently hoped it was Turk. If whatever it was decided that it wasn't Turk and wanted to hurt me, it would probably pinch me in half at the waist.

Okay, I wasn't thinking too clearly. So what else is new?

"Okay, Harry. We've got you!"

"Great!" I would have said that I had thought they already (expletive deleted) had me, otherwise I wouldn't have let go of the (expletive deleted) ladder, but I thought they might take the ingratitude personally and let go of the rope. Funny how your mind works in situations like this.

Then gravity grabbed hold of me, and I landed hard. Something roughly the mass of a small mastodon, or my security officer, landed harder right on top of me, and a buzzing sound filled my ears. The blackness fled from my faceplate as eager hands lifted the crushing weight from me and pulled me to my feet.

Someone removed my helmet, and someone else started at the seals of the suit, but I waved them off. Removing the suit in the privacy of my own cabin seemed like a good idea, all things considered. Zook was waving a graviton emitter over Turk, who was lying on the deck, still struggling to breathe. His face was shifting from blue to pink fairly quickly. Other than that, he looked like crap. There were a lot of tears in his jumper, and some in his skin.

I took a double take, and realized that he wasn't bleeding.

Two of his security team were searching through a first-aid kit, but since there was no blood, the coag-patches weren't really necessary. There was a bit of mumbling, and someone said something about Sploig, but the tears in the skin were not closing, at least not quickly, and there were bits of metal and other machinery showing through the gaps. Evidently, I wasn't the only one onboard with a few prosthetics.

Maybe that explains all of his ex-wives.

"What the hell happened?" he asked, looking around the cramped airlock at all the worried faces.

"You don't remember?" Zook asked, sounding disappointed that Turk wouldn't be giving us a first-hand account of his experience.

"I remember Charley yelling something down at me, but it went all dark, and I couldn't hang on to my weapon." He looked down at his hands, obviously disappointed that he'd dropped his linguini blaster. "I lost it, didn't I?"

For a moment I thought he was either going to cry or jump up and dive through the hatch after his lost toy.

"I'll buy you a new one," I said, unclipping the rope from my suit and grinning down at him. "But next time you hear someone say 'All aboard', get your ass up the ladder and into the airlock, okay?"

"Yeah," he said. He looked down at the holes his jumper and the tears in his skin. "Looks like I got chewed up some, huh."

"Uh, Turk?" I asked, trying to stay calm. "What's with the metal and wires and stuff under your skin?"

Yes, as a matter of fact, "Tact" *is* my middle name.

"Oh, that. Well, you know how I was in the Marines, right?" We all nodded numbly, having heard far too many times about Turk's exploits in the Galactic Marine Corps. They aren't really much more than mercenaries, you know. Contracting out grunt military might is one of Earth-Gov's only means of legitimate income. There's always someone fighting somewhere in the galaxy, and there will always be brave young men and women willing to risk their lives for the chance of fame, fortune, and the opportunity to shoot some really neat guns.

I guess I missed out on that typically macho gene. Bummer…

"Well, my last mission was on Carpathia Prime, and we were taking some killer incoming artillery fire." We all tried to look interested, but this could take hours. "Artie had a bead on our CP, so we were doing a down and dirty until the fly-boys could bail our bacon out of the fire. Then there was—"

"Uh, Turk?" I hated to interrupt—not really—but I needed to change clothes…soon.

"Oh, sorry, Harry. Well, the short story is that I kinda got blown up." He shrugged, as if mentioning that he'd clipped his toenails a little too close.

"Blown up?" I had to ask.

"Yeah. I got the scoop from my buddies afterward." He shrugged again, managing to sit up. I noticed that a lot of the holes in his skin had already closed up. Nice trick. "I caught a round of artillery right about here." He poked himself in the stomach. "They scraped up what they could find, stuffed it in a casualty bag and sent it off to the medics. I woke up with all this hardware."

"I've never seen prosthetics like this." I cocked an eyebrow skeptically, then asked Zook for an explanation. "You ever see prosthetics like this?"

"I have never seen prosthetics like this, Harry." He looked closely at one of the gashes in Turk's hide that was closing up. "Who did the work?"

"Uh, I thought the docs at the VA hospital, but…" Zook gave a snort of laughter. "No, huh?"

"That is not very likely, Turk." Zook looked at me like a kid with a new toy. "This is some really sophisticated work, Harry. Can I take some samples? Please?"

"Ask Turk."

Zook looked to Turk and helped him to his feet.

"What kind of samples?"

"Well, some skin would be a good start, and I'd love to do some scans. How much of you is you, and how much is prosthetic?"

Turk looked a little affronted, then embarrassed. "Well, most of my head is me, I think," he said, looking up as if he could look inside his own skull. "And my left foot, and some of my right." He bit his lip, thinking. "Oh, and my left index finger."

"You're kidding, right?" I asked, giving him a carefully tailored scowl of disbelief. I looked to Zook for help. "He's kidding, right?"

"I don't know, Harry." He pinched a bit of exposed skin, and Turk grimaced and glared.

"Hey, that hurt!"

"Interesting…" Zook reached out to pinch again, but Turk slapped his hand away.

"Stop that! And no, you can't have any samples!" He glared at the whole group. "Stop staring! I'm fine."

"Okay, that's enough," I ordered, waving the crowd out the door. "Everyone back to your stations. We'll be jumping back to Earth in just a few minutes. I'll be on the bridge in half an hour. Don't shift the ship into real space until I get there, okay, Kik?" I turned to go to my stateroom to get cleaned up.

"Sure, Harry."

"Uh, and thanks, Harry," Turk said, evidently noticing my spacesuit and doing the math in his head, which was impressive considering the source. "For coming out after me, I mean."

"Don't mention it, Turk," I said, honestly hoping he wouldn't. I didn't want to be reminded of my own stupidity, and gratitude from someone like Turk made me uncomfortable. He'd probably try to thank me by teaching me how to shoot or something. Not that marksmanship wouldn't be a handy skill, but I doubt I'd have the patience to learn anything from Turk.

Cleaning up didn't take as long as I thought it would, since the damage wasn't as extensive as I'd feared. One advantage to all the running around was that I didn't get to have my morning coffee, or at least it's an advantage when something literally scares the bodily fluids out of you. The cleaning bill would be only for my jumper, not the spacesuit. Considering how often I went through jumpers, between embracing Carpoolians, getting spattered by exploding Farfnian mudpuppies, and firefights in disreputable restaurants, my laundry bill probably wouldn't be affected in the least.

My big surprise when I got to the bridge was that Turk was there. I don't know why, but after his ordeal I thought he'd take some time to recover. Okay, so maybe I'm wrong about these things a lot, but at least I'm consistent.

"What are you doing here, Turk?" I asked, eying him professionally. He looked fine, but it's so hard to tell with Turk. "You sure you're feeling up to standing a watch?"

"I'm fine, Harry," he said, leveling a glare across the bridge to where Zook sat. Zook, in turn, was looking at Turk like a kid with a science project and a new set of tools. My guess was that they'd had a few heated words in my absence.

"Now children, play nice," I muttered, taking my seat. I don't think either of them heard me. "Well, Zook, do we know where we'll be when we pop back into real space?"

"Considering who was outside the ship when we shifted, we should end up back in the Sploig bubble world or in New Jersey."

"New Jersey?"

"What's wrong with New Jersey?" Turk rumbled in the tone that made my bones ache.

"Oh, nothing! Nothing!" I lied, wondering which of Zook's possible destinations I would rather end up in. "It's uh…well…it's on Earth, at least. That's an advantage."

"Everybody thinks Jersey's some kinda dump. Newark's a *nice* town!"

"I'm sure it is, Turk," I said, trying not to sound condescending. "Well, Kik, just be ready to shift us back into stringspace if we end up someplace unfriendly."

"Right, Harry." She dropped her clothes and slid into the pilot's couch.

I've decided that I believe in reincarnation, and I'm lobbying big-time with any deity that will listen to come back as a pilot's couch. Well, okay, knowing my luck, I'd come back as Bubba the Love Sponge's pilot couch. Oh, never mind.

I plugged myself in, just to have a tight link with Kik if we ended up in someplace horrible, like Newark, and had to shift out quickly. "Everyone ready?" I asked, knowing what I'd get, but not wanting to miss a chance to make my lowly crew feel important. You know, pep up morale a bit.

"Ready Harry," Turk rumbled in his bone-rattling tone.

"Oh yes, we are ready, Harry. Though I don't know if the *Limburger* is. With all the damage she has taken, it would be best if we didn't make a reentry approach. Burning up in the atmosphere would be a new experience for me, but one that I don't believe you would—"

"I'll tell Kik to keep it slow." Remind me to add *chatty Immortal* to my list of dislikes. I opened the intercom and told my crew to hang on, then gave Kik the go ahead.

"Okay, Harry. Here we go."

I felt that strange little shift inside that told me we'd made the jump out of stringspace, but nothing else happened. The viewer was still blank, the comm system was still dead, and my conscience still refused to make me feel bad about the Twinkie I'd put on Ms. Krznowski's chair in the second grade. Some things are worth two years of detention.

"Turk?"

"Uh, well, I don't think we're in Newark."

"Well, that's a relief anyway." And some things are worth broken bones. "Zook, are we still in stringspace?"

"I don't think so, Harry. We shifted to somewhere, but I just don't know where." He worked a few controls at his console, then shrugged. "Everything I send out bounces back with no data. We're not in stringspace, but I can't tell you that we are in real space either. It's like we're in a bubble."

I didn't like the sound of that.

"I don't like the sound of that," I said, letting the crew in on things for a change. "We're someplace we don't want to be, Kik. Shift us back to stringspace."

"Right, Harry."

Nothing happened. No jolt. No nothing.

"Kik?"

"I know, Harry. The field won't form up. It's like there's not enough room around the ship, but—"

A knife blade of light swept through the ship from top to bottom, slicing through everything as it passed. I felt a little warm rush as it lashed through my skull, but nothing bad happened. At least, I didn't start reciting sports statistics or anything. That generally only happens when I get X-rayed, but Zook says he's working on fixing that glitch.

"What the hell was that?" Turk's shout hurt worse than the light.

"Harry, what just happened?" Kik asked.

"We have just been scanned," Zook informed us, and I passed the information to Kik, "right down to our molecular structures. Quite sophisticated." He was grinning again, damn him.

"What's so entertaining, Zook?"

"The scan. It answers many questions."

"It does?" It seemed to me that it posed many more than it answered, but I'm the 'Huh?' type, not the 'Aha!' type.

"Oh, yes, Harry!"

"Does it answer the one about where the hell we are?" Turk was showing his usual amount of patience.

"Uh, no, not really, but it explains where *you* came from."

"Me? I came from Newark!"

"Well, yes, you originally came from Newark, but after your injury, much of you was replaced. I think this is where that was done."

"Huh?" See, I told you I was the 'Huh?' type.

"And I think I know who, or at least what, did it."

"What?" Turk must be the 'What?' type.

The forward viewer suddenly flooded with light, as if a hundred spotlights were being shone right in a window. I raised a hand against the glare. A shape was silhouetted against the light, and it was walking toward the ship. I heard the pilot's couch open, and Kik's exclamation at the spectacle.

"Well, I hope whoever did it is friendly."

"Oh, I think he is friendly, Harry."

"Well, if they're not, we're screwed. I can't even get a reading on the engines, let alone fire them. The whole drive system's dead." Kik didn't sound like she shared Zook's optimism.

As the figure approached I caught glimpses of shadows cluttering the area around the ship. Many were machines, other ships, and some other things that looked half machine-half alive. And I was wearing my last clean jumper…damn.

"Well, should we open the hatch?" I asked, as Turk rummaged through his toy chest for an appropriately dangerous device. Somehow I knew it wouldn't do us any good, even if he had another linguini blaster tucked away in there.

"I don't think that will be—"

Zook didn't finish because it became quite obvious that I didn't need to open a door to let our host inside the ship.

As the figure got closer, an all-too-human figure, I might add, the light behind it dimmed. When it got close enough to fill the viewer, it shimmered and was standing right in front of the viewer, on the *inside* of the ship! On the bridge!

A dumpy little man in brown overalls smiled at us as his twinkling eyes surveyed the bridge. His gaze settled on each of us in turn, and his mouth quirked into a strangely familiar smile. Finally his gaze settled on Turk.

"So, Turk, how's the bod holdin' up?"

"Uh, good, Sparky. Thanks."

"Sparky?" I asked, cocking an eyebrow at Turk. I'd have fired it at him, too, but I rarely keep my eyebrows loaded.

"You *know* him?" Kik asked, finally finding the composure to slip into her jumper. That was when I realized that Sparky wasn't human, or even your run-of-the-mill alien; his gaze hadn't lingered on Kik any more than it had on any of us.

"Uh, yeah. He's Sparky Portman, the tech specialist from my old unit."

"I never thought of joining the Marines. It must have been interesting." Zook sounded strange, like he was embarrassed or something.

"Oh, it was! Gave me all kinda opportunities to patch stuff up. Like Turk here!" He walked over to Turk and patted him on the chest. "Gooder'n new!"

"You're an Immortal," I said, trying not to slur my words with the realization.

"An Immortal with bad grammar," Kik added, earning a chuckle from Sparky.

"Haw, haw! She's a pert li'l thang ain't she?" He looked her up and down and shrugged. "I suppose I could talk like ya'll, if it would help you sleep better, Kikira, but I don't get to talk to much of anybody round here, so I guess I'm a mite out of practice."

"How long?" Zook asked, stepping over to his kinsman.

"Well, after I left Turk's unit, I settled back down here to tinker with some stuff. Time flies when you're tinkerin', you know."

"Fourteen years?" Turk asked, cocking his own eyebrows. His probably *were* loaded.

"Sounds about right."

"I am surprised you're still alive." Zook took a step closer and held out his hand. "Shall we?"

"Well, I suppose."

The two shook hands and smiled at one another.

"Do you two know each other?" Kik asked.

"We do now," Sparky said with a laugh.

"Yes, we most certainly do." Zook sighed with a smile like I hadn't ever seen on him. "Nice meeting you, Sparky."

"You, too, Zook." He turned and walked toward the view screen, talking as he went. "I shut down the shield and freed up yer ship's systems. You might want to head on outta here." He looked over his shoulder one last time and said, "I've gotten kinda used to my privacy, ya know."

"Uh, sure," I said, feeling like I at least should say something. Sparky walked right through the front view screen of my bridge, and I sat down. I was feeling a little thick-headed. "Kik, have a seat and shift us back into stringspace, please."

"Sure, Harry." She got back into the couch and, before I could even warn the crew, I felt the jolt of the ship shifting back into stringspace. It almost felt like home after that little incident.

"Well, that was weird," I managed, slouching down in my seat as Kik got back out and got dressed.

"I'll say!" Turk agreed. "And the weirdest part was finding out I've got an alien body!" He poked himself in the middle and frowned. "I kinda feel like I'm gonna barf."

"Don't worry about it, Turk. You'll get used to the idea." I tapped my head with a finger.

"Can we go home now?" Kik asked, glaring at the rest of us. "I'm getting tired of taking my clothes off and having to put them right back on again."

"Yes, we can go home now, Kik. Just let me get something from my cabin and throw it out the airlock, and we'll be home."

"You brought something from The Barn?" Turk asked, his spirits perking up.

"Yeah, a little patch of clover from the first floor pasture. Should get us back right on the mark."

"Good," Zook said, slouching in his couch. "I'm not feeling very well."

"Huh? Why not?"

"Oh, it will pass," he said with a strange smile. "But it will feel good to be home."

"And I imagine Tom and the other Tillamookers are driving the CEO crazy by now," Kik added with a wry chuckle.

"Damn, I hadn't thought of that." I got up and headed for my cabin. I guess I really should have planned on getting back before they got there, but why should I start thinking ahead at this point?

CHAPTER THIRTEEN

THE BIG CHEESE

Considering the means of our departure, I probably should have guessed that the CEO would be a little more than mildly irritated with me when I got back. I guess I was just too euphoric to think unhappy thoughts. We'd accomplished everything we set out to do on this trip and then some. We'd saved Tillamook, or at least its inhabitants, discovered a new and immensely powerful alien threat, and even got a piece of their technology. And we hadn't even had to use our holdful of cheese as barter. On top of that, I'd discovered that my ex-girlfriend was in fact not a girl at all, but a shape-shifting alien, which made me feel perversely better about being dumped. Consequently, I was in a positively stellar mood and wasn't thinking much about the consequences of my earlier actions. But you've been listening to me long enough to know that I'm not big on thinking ahead.

Honestly, with all we've been through, I was feeling lucky to be alive. I've decided that I'd rather be lucky than good.

So, when we popped in on the first floor pasture of the Wisconsin Cheese Company and only managed to scare the crap out of a herd of dairy cows, I wasn't particularly surprised. Nobody watches the pasture levels. There are cameras, of course, but watching cows eat grass is almost as boring as watching ENN without the commercials, so nobody really pays much attention to the screens. They probably wouldn't even know we were here until we walked in the back door.

"Set her down easy, Kik," I said through my link, running a quick diagnostic on the *Limburger's* systems. "No need to scare the herd more than necessary." Dairy cows don't handle stress well. They'd probably be giving cottage cheese for two days.

Kik muttered something about not having to deal with micro-managing captains before I was hardwired into the *Limburger*, but I ignored her. She was obviously delirious with the joy of our safe return, and wasn't making much sense. She was, however, still a damn fine pilot, and put the ship down as light as a feather.

I finished my system check just as Kik shut down the engines, popped the couch and reached for her jumper. She was in remarkably good condition. The ship, not Kik, although she certainly is, too.

How about needlepoint for a hobby? Nah.

Except for an alien minivan jammed up through the cargo lift door and a few scratches around the landing gear, she was ready for her next run. All things considered, I'd take the damaged lift; that Sploigmobile was worth its weight in cheese.

"All hands," I said over the shipwide intercom, "we are officially home-again, home-again. Feel free to leave your seats and move freely around the ship." I thought about the *lucky to be alive* thing again and added, "Your captain will be in the bar. If you wish to join him, he will be buying drinks for his crew until exactly next week. This is Captain Harry Fische, signing off."

"What was that all about?" Kik asked, sealing the last of her Velcro and starting with her boots.

"Oh, just feeling lucky," I said, not really expecting her to get it. I guess I always get this giddy exhilaration when I've finished a run, although this run wasn't exactly a run in the conventional sense. But we were alive. Big plus. "Wanna join me for a drink, Kik?" She stared at me for a bit without answering. I guess she was a little stunned. "How about you, Turk? A yard of ale sound good?"

"Sounds great, Harry. Thanks!"

"Zook, how about you. Join us?"

"I don't think so, Harry, but thank you for the offer." He looked a little strange—I mean, stranger than he usually does. Most people don't notice that Zook looks different than any other human. I guess it's more his mannerisms than his physical appearance, but I've been around him a lot and I know when he's feeling off. Usually his moods end up with me sitting up with him all night trying to talk him out of creative means of suicide, but this was different.

"You okay, Zook? You look a little pale." He didn't really, but it was a good opener.

"Oh, I am okay, Harry. Just a little tired. I will be fine in—" he looked at his chronometer, "three months, six days, four hours, and sixteen minutes or so."

"Huh?" This was weird even for Zook. "What's with the countdown?"

"Nothing, Harry. I'm just not quite feeling myself." He smiled in that way I'd only seen once before, when he was shaking hands with Sparky. Usually when he smiles we're about to die. "I'll stay with the *Limburger*."

"You're sure?" Zook never really drank much anyway. Not your usual depressed suicidal, I know.

"I'll be fine, Harry." He smiled that smile again, creeping me out thoroughly.

"Okay, then. See you in a few hours. We'll probably have to move the ship to the hanger soon. I'm sure the cows don't like it."

"Right, Harry. I'll be here." He waved as Kik, Turk and I left the bridge.

The lift was still out of service, so it took a few minutes to get to the airlock, and I worried about Zook all the way. He seemed different, almost happy, and when his life wasn't even in danger. That was weird for Zook.

We filed down the airlock ladder with the rest of the crew amid many jests and hand-shaking thanks for my magnanimous offer. Even Mishi was in a good mood, though I passed on his offer for a handshake; I'd forgotten my oven mitt. It was a short walk across the pasture, avoiding the interspersed lumps of steaming cow droppings that were evidence that we had indeed frightened the herd into unexpected bowel motility. I glanced at the nervous cows as we approached the doors to the processing level, hoping we hadn't scared them too badly. I pressed my palm to the lock on the processing-room doors and wondered where the cows from Tillamook had been housed.

The door opened, and I found out.

"Holy cow!" Mishi shouted, just as seventy very nervous Guernseys surged through the door, right into my more-than-slightly-astonished crew.

"Hey! Close that door!" someone shouted over the din of anxious bovines and equally anxious cheese runners. Someone else yelped as they fell beneath the bovine onslaught. I tried to grab Kik, but an angry cow butted me aside. She swore, but I saw that Turk had her. He simply lifted her up with one hand and batted a few of the charging slabs of beef out of the way with the other. I didn't have Turk's mass or his nerve, but I managed to stay on my feet, shouting expletives and swatting at very large wet noses as they tried to insert themselves into my chest.

The herd wasn't really panicked, which undoubtedly saved lives, but they wanted out of the processing hold, and we were in the way. Most of the crew managed to dash to the left or right, but several of us had been standing front and center. The whole stampede lasted less time than it takes to wonder about the irony of surviving being captured by shape-shifting aliens, then dying under the hooves of a herd of angry milk cows. I know because I was thinking exactly that when the very last bovine in the procession bowled me over and stepped right on my arm.

And it didn't even moo in apology.

I was too busy swearing at the pain and trying to get back to my feet to notice what people were saying around me. Then something hard was being jammed into my chest and someone said, "Just stay there, Fische! You're under arrest!"

I opened my eyes and noticed that the something sticking me in the ribs was the business end of a rifle, and that the person doing the sticking was the one I least wanted to see.

"Oh. Hi, Chief." I levered myself up to one elbow and grimaced at the pain in the other one. It felt like Turk had gotten hold of it. "What's with the gun? You expecting an invasion or something?"

"We've already *had* an invasion, thanks to you, Fische! And those cows you just set loose were under quarantine! Now they're mixing with our herd and transmitting who knows what kind of infections." He punctuated the last with another jab in the ribs with the muzzle of his gun, a practice that I was beginning to dislike very quickly. "That's why you're under arrest, along with a long string of similar traitorous violations!"

"Traitorous?" That was Turk, somewhere to my left. He sounded upset. That wasn't good. I didn't want him to do something foolish, like kill my boss. Well, okay, maybe I wanted it a little.

That was when I noticed several WCC security goons standing around with weapons pointed at the rest of my crew. It crossed my mind to ask what the hell was going on, but even more pressing at that moment was the bone in my forearm that was threatening to punch through the fabric of my jumper sleeve. It seemed to be broken quite badly.

"Yes, traitorous!" the CEO shouted, jabbing again. "He melted one of our ion cannons, gave away secret frequencies to our competitors, and now has released quarantined animals into our herd. If that's not treason, I don't know what is."

"Fine! Arrest me then, but if you don't get me to a medical unit soon, my (expletive deleted) arm is going to fall off!" I levered myself to my feet, enduring two more pokes with his rifle, which did nothing for my temper. More than a couple of my crew needed medical attention worse than me. Maybe my luck was spent, but at that point I wasn't about to put up with this kind of stupidity, especially with my arm in splinters and my ego on the line. "And if you don't stop poking me in the ribs with that gun, I'm going to let Turk jam it up your ass and pull the trigger!"

I really shouldn't let my ego do the talking. It's not very smart.

But the CEO must have taken me seriously. He cast a worried glance toward Turk, who was, I assumed, looking adequately pissed-off to instill fear in a seasoned combat veteran. My ego was counting on the fact that the Chief was a paper pusher, not a soldier. I don't know if it was the pain in my arm, or the utter inanity of the whole situation that prompted me to do it, but the next thing I knew, I'd grabbed the muzzle of his rifle, pushed it up, and planted a kick squarely where his legs met his pelvis.

The gun went off, blasting a sizable hole in the ceiling, probably inducing more bovine bowel motility, and maybe even some human and alien. The CEO's eyes widened, then crossed and rolled up. He crumpled like a rented tux on a wedding night, leaving me holding his gun by the barrel in my one good hand, and staring at twenty armed security goons who were gaping at me like I'd just spontaneously combusted.

"You can't do that!" one exclaimed. "You're under arrest!"

I tossed the rifle aside and referred to the excrement of male bovines. "If I'm under arrest, then take me into custody for cripes sake!" I waved my hand at the members of my crew who were injured and said, "And get them to medical…right…now…" I'd waved the wrong hand, and now my forearm was bent at a right angle between my elbow and wrist.

"Well, crap, would you look at that," I said. I didn't know that my prosthetic brain would let me faint, but everything got very dark all of the sudden, and the next thing I knew I was lying on top of the CEO.

He wasn't very comfortable.

***

It took the medical robots almost a half hour to fix my arm, a testament that it was well and truly broken, and that I wasn't a sissy for having fainted. Well, that's what they told me, anyway, and I never argue with doctors, even robotic ones. Not that they're never wrong, mind you, they just never admit it.

Needless to say, being arrested put a bit of a damper on our celebration. I hoped that the crew wasn't too upset. The goon squad had only arrested the bridge crew, so the rest of them didn't have too much to be upset about. In fact, as I was getting out of medical, they were probably on their second round and charging it to my tab. I was escorted to the detention block—I didn't even know we had one—and joined Turk, Kik and the officers of the Tillamook ships. We were a little crowded.

"Sorry about this, Tom," I said, shrugging helplessly as the door clanged closed behind me. "I didn't think the Chief would be such a twit about the whole thing."

"Not your fault, Fische. You can't help it if the guy's a dick." He shook my hand and grinned. "He can't keep us locked up forever, and he ain't likely to turn up his nose at seventy head of dairy cows and ten new ships. Though we might have pushed the facilities a bit. Not much parking left in the hanger, I'm afraid."

"They said something about holding an inquest," one of the captains said. "Said the CEO had been hurt in the stampede, but as soon as he's on his feet, everyone's going to be called to a meeting."

"That should be an interesting meeting," I said, wondering if kicking the CEO in the huevos was not such a great idea after all.

"Yeah. Kikira here told us what you did to him." Tom snickered. "That took some balls, Harry."

"Yeah, the Chief's," Turk put in, clapping me on the shoulder like I'd passed some rite of machoism.

"Well, it seemed like the thing to do at the time, and I'm sure I got points for spontaneity."

"At least he's not a Sploig," Kik said, smiling. "Though I don't think your method of testing will help us out at the inquest."

"It's not like I did anything against the WCC bylaws by rearranging his testicles with my foot. There are no rules specifically against it, and he's not likely to bring me up on assault charges with the local Farfnian Law Enforcement." I wasn't going to mention that he had me dead to rights on the other stuff, though I would argue about damaging the ion cannon during our departure. He *was* trying to shoot us, so it was self-defense, right?

"What's the worst he could do to us?" Tom asked, looking slightly less worried than when he found out twenty of his people had been replaced by Sploig.

"Kick us out on our keisters, I guess." I didn't relish the thought of being out in the world without a job, a place to live, or any means of supporting myself, but it wasn't like I wouldn't have any company. Most of the population of Earth is in the same boat. Well, public housing isn't so bad, or so they say.

"I guess we could take our ships and try to make a living hauling legitimate cargo." He shrugged. "Don't seem the same, though."

"Uh, yeah, well, he probably wouldn't let you leave with your ships, Tom." His mouth fell open. I thought of reaching up and closing it for him, but I didn't know how he'd take it. "Sorry about that."

Angry murmurs spread through the tightly packed crowd, all directed to me. There were a lot of accusations, some outright threats and one proposition to rearrange my internal organs, but the gist of it was that they were not *particularly* happy. Yeah, and politicians aren't *particularly* honest…

"Now hang on a second," Turk rumbled, quelling the crowd's ire.

Turk's good at quelling ire. He's kind of like a really big ire hydrant. All you have to do is latch onto him with a few lines and… Oh, fine, but it was a good pun, you must admit. Anyway, he defended my efforts to save the Tillamookers, and since he could have mopped up the entire detention block with one hand, they couldn't very well disagree with him or threaten him or threaten me. Yes, Turk definitely has his uses.

"Don't worry, Tom. It's not going to go that far. The Chief would be an idiot to cut you loose."

"I would?" a rather stern voice said from behind me.

Crap.

Well, in for a penny in for a pound, I always say. Well, not really. In fact I hardly ever say that, but it just seemed to fit the moment. Anyway, with that phrase in mind, I turned to my erstwhile employer and said, "Yes, Chief, you would."

His face turned that color, the one I mentioned before.

"You must know that you're out of here, Fische. What makes you think you can bring in these strangers and take over? This is *my* organization. I run things here and you broke the rules. You're gone!"

"Am I?" I looked down as if I expected to see myself fading away. "That's funny, I don't feel gone." I guess I was working under the premise that the madder I could make him, the more likely he would be to do something stupid. Well, it works on me.

"This is ridiculous! The sooner we get this over with, the sooner I don't have to listen to your crap any longer." He waved his goon squad forward. "Get them to the auditorium." He turned and stalked off, madder than ever.

"Were you *trying* to piss him off?" Tom asked, his own temper escalating from simmer to boil.

"Was it that obvious?" I asked back as the guards ushered us out of the holding cell. "I guess I need to work on my subtlety."

"But why?" Tom was obviously taken aback by my tactic—or lack thereof.

"Just wait and see, Tom." I smiled knowingly. It wasn't like I had the slightest inkling of a plan or anything, but I did know that the rest of cheese fleet would be there. Corporate decisions of this type aren't made without a quorum; that *is* in the bylaws.

We were escorted to the auditorium with Kik, Turk, and the Tillamook crews in tow. The scene reminded me of the previous meeting, the room crowded to standing room only with the command crews of forty or so ships in audience. There were security guards all over the place waving around more guns than Turk had in his whole closet.

The CEO's amplified voice boomed out over the crowd, filing the charges and calling for a vote for immediate termination of H. Fische and his mutinous crew. Relax, he meant termination like a pink slip, not like a noose and gallows.

As the echo of his rant died away, one of the captains called a point of order.

"The Chairman recognizes Marty Stenson, Captain of the *Emmenthaler*." I had no idea why the Chief was talking about himself in third person like that, but I had to smile.

"We'd like to hear Harry's side of it," Marty said, which got a murmur from the crowd. "Let him talk."

"Anything he's got to say is irrelevant!" the chief started, but someone else shouted, "Second the motion!"

164

"All in favor?"

The CEO opened his mouth to object, but the room was swept with a murmur of "Ayes".

"Opposed?"

"Damn right I oppose this ridiculous suggestion! He's a damned traitor to this company, and could have gotten us squashed by the Farfnians!"

"But he didn't!" The owner of the voice that had seconded the motion stepped forward; it was Meredith Grendler. She glared down the two security goons who stepped in front of her and said, "And a motion has been passed. Let him talk."

The room rumbled with assent. The CEO looked a little worried, especially at the way his security men had melted away from Meri's onslaught. Not that it would ever come down to an actual fight, but his goon squad was outnumbered about eight to one, and it was a safe bet that a good number of the cheese runners were armed. He obviously realized this and wasn't about to try to stand up against the pressure.

"Fine! The accused will be given the floor for a *short* explanation of his actions."

Oh boy! A floor of my very own! I thought. And, no, I have no idea where these things come from. I guess I'm just a terminal smart-ass.

I smiled and winked at Tom before I stood up, but he seemed more worried than before.

"Thanks, Chief. I'll try to be brief."

He just glared at me, but I saw the corner of Meredith's mouth twitch. This was going to be fun.

"First, I'd like to make it clear that my crew and officers were following my orders, and shouldn't be held responsible for any of the damage done to the Chief's expensive ion cannon." I got a smile from Kik on that one, which made it completely worthwhile. "At the time, we were hovering the ship so we could jump into stringspace and not take out any of the other ships parked next to us. If he hadn't charged, and in fact *fired* on my ship, there would have been no damage to anything. I knew our activation of the jump field wasn't likely to attract attention. I tried to explain that to the Chief at the time, but he wasn't listening. You know how he gets."

That got a light chuckle from a few of the assembled crews, and a serious scowl from the CEO; exactly what I'd hoped for.

"Second, I knew from my engineer, Zook, that Tillamook had been stolen, not pulverized. The evidence was obvious enough for anyone who wanted to believe it." I looked sidelong at the Chief, squinting with suspicion. "Which makes one wonder why he didn't *want* to believe it… But let's not play the blame game here.

"The fact is, we went to bring Tillamook back, and we did. If anyone doubts that, check out the *new* crater where Tillamook used to be. I doubt that ENN will broadcast the pictures, but we can hack into the satellite feed easily enough. What you'll see is a *real* impact crater, probably still smoking. We did get the Tillamookers back, and saved their ships, crews and some of their herd, but we couldn't keep the crabs from dropping a rock on the factory.

"Third, and much more importantly, we discovered exactly *who* stole Tillamook, and why."

I paused here for effect. I really should have majored in drama in school, but girls were so much more interesting. Too bad they don't give you a degree for that.

"But if you'd all rather vote me terminated, I'll take my recordings of the Sploig mobile home world and my samples of their superior technology—superior to us *and* the Farfnians, mind you—and I'll go sell it to the *French*."

Mayhem, outbursts, shouts, and general cacophony erupted.

Order was returned by the CEO hammering the microphone with his fist and shouting "Order!" I thought of voicing my desire for a cheeseburger and fries, but realized it probably wouldn't help us much.

"All this is hearsay! He's got no evidence!"

Tom shouted a term we often use to refute that which we believe to be false. Strange, isn't it, since there's very little doubt, when a bull does that particular thing that bulls do, that it's quite real?

"If it's fabrication, where the hell did we come from?"

"You're in cahoots with him!"

Just for the record, I've never been in a cahoot in my life. I almost was once, but we found a motel room instead.

"He staged this to bring his own bought-and-paid-for crews here and undercut our prices! He's here to take over WCC, and I won't have it!"

Silence enveloped the auditorium like a soft, secure blanket. It was hard for me not to smile at his outburst, but I managed to only look astonished. No, really!

"Uh, yeah. Now that we've got that out in the open, would anyone here mind if I just showed you all what we found out there?"

Murmurs of assent swept the room.

"He's crazy!" the Chief bellowed. "He's got some light show cooked up!"

"I move to allow Harry to show us what he's found," Meredith rumbled dangerously. She could give Turk a run for his money in the intimidation department.

The move was seconded and passed before the CEO could put his foot in his mouth again.

"Okay, I need a comm unit. I didn't bring mine."

"Crap, Harry, what kind of captain are you?" Meredith said, elbowing her way to the podium and handing over hers.

"I thought I was going to a bar to celebrate, not to some kind of inquisition. Thanks, Meredith." I tuned the thing and said, "Zook, you there?"

"Yes, Harry, I'm here."

"How much have you learned from the Sploigmobile?" I knew he couldn't resist playing with the thing as soon as we were off the ship.

"Well, quite a lot, actually. Some of the technology is quite impressive! Did you know that they can use a perpetuating meson field generator to—"

"Did you figure out how they made the robossassins teleport?"

"Oh, yes, Harry. That was easy."

"Okay, good. Can you send me something that I can patch into my brain so I can project my memories of the Sploig bubble world to the angry ladies and gentlemen that the CEO has brought together to decide whether or not to fire me and the crew, so that just maybe they won't fire us and force me to ask you to blow the *Limburger* into smithereens?" Deep breath on my part, and much muttering from the crowd followed my simple request.

"Oh, uh…sure, Harry. Give me a minute." The link went dead. Great.

You ever time a minute when people are pointing guns at you? It's a looooog time…

Tick tock.

Ho hum…

Forty five seconds…

"Ahem!!" That was the chief…

"Just a second."

"This is ridiculous! I put forth a mandatory vote on whether or not we should expel Harry and his cockeyed crew from this corporation! All those in favor, say— Holy crap!"

Thankfully, very few people echoed his exclamation as the robossassin materialized two feet in front of the podium.

Turk pulled two handguns, did a diving roll and came up with both aimed at the thing. Kik just said, "Uh-oh", and the rest of the room gasped and brought a plethora of weaponry to bear. But the robossassin just turned and held out a little wire with a plug that looked very familiar.

"Everybody just hold your fire! This nice robossassin has obviously been reprogrammed by my engineer. I didn't even know there were any in the vehicle we…uh…captured."

"Captured?" Kik whispered with a smirk.

"Hey, go with it! I'm ad-libbing here!" I stepped forward. "Now, let me demonstrate…" I took the wire, having absolutely no idea what would happen when I plugged myself into the thing. For all I knew it would eat my brain and take over Earth, only able to be stopped by a sexy female saying "Klatu-Barada-Nicto."

What, you never saw that movie? Oh, man! It's a classic!

Anyway, I plugged in, and the robossassin's eyes projected a hologram into the center of the bowl-shaped room. There were quite a few gasps and mutters of "What the hell is he doing?" Not too many people knew I had a computer for a brain, and even fewer knew I could plug in. I guess it's kind of a shock to find out someone's not quite all human.

Or maybe the gasps of astonishment were for something else.

I looked up at the hologram that was projecting exactly what I was thinking of at that moment.

I was a little embarrassed to see Kik climbing out of the pilot's couch right there for everyone to see, but I changed channels really quickly. I don't think she saw it. Well, maybe not... She didn't hit me anyway.

The next view was of The Inferno, as the robossassins blinked in and blasted Neezl to slimy little bits. I fast-forwarded, explaining our rushed departure, the chase with the Sploigmobile, and how Zook saved our bacon.

Then everyone got a good look at the Sploig and what they really were. There were exclamations of disbelief and a few of astonishment, and even more of outright terror. I knew how they felt. The bit with Kik being enveloped and falling into the blackness of stringspace was a real crowd-pleaser. Well, it got their attention.

Then there was the bubble world...

That achieved astonished silence.

I love it when I have a crowd in the palm of my hand. Not that it's ever happened since then, mind you, but I love it.

I ran my memories forward to the point where we blinked out from under the falling asteroid. The rest was personal, and I knew Turk would break quite a few of my bones if I showed the whole WCC that he was a cyborg. He had my sympathy there.

I pulled the plug and said, "Well, that's about it." I handed the wire back to the robossassin, and said, "You can go back to the *Limburger* now." It nodded and vanished.

Nice theatre, Zook. Very nice.

"Anyway," I said, shrugging nonchalantly, "that's a taste of what the Sploig are. We brought back some of their technology. If we use it, we've got a chance. They're not going to be happy that we stole Tillamook and ruined their plans."

The room was pretty quiet, considering there were about two hundred people whispering to one another all at once.

The CEO called for order, twice. He was about to do so a third time when Meredith bellowed over him a motion to adjourn this inquest. It was seconded about fifty times and the "All in favor say—" was met with such a resounding "AYE" by the whole room that I really started to feel good about myself.

I turned to Tom and said. "That means we're off the hook."

"Ya think?" he quipped with that doofy Oregonian grin of his.

I grinned right back, just as doofily, no doubt.

Meredith once again broke through the din with another bellowed motion. I think she could have been an opera singer, if she'd applied her ability to project to a more melodious form. Uh-huh.

It was the motion that left me with my mouth hanging open.

"I put forth a motion that we vote right now on a new CEO for the Wisconsin Cheese Company Incorporated!"

"You what?" I asked, but I was drowned out by the seconds and the ayes… "Wait, Meri, I don't want to—"

"I nominate Harry Fische!" someone shouted. I was looking for the bastard who said it so I could tell Turk to shoot him, but once again I was lost in the flurry of seconds.

"Wait a second! I don't want—"

"Shut up, Harry! There's a motion on the floor. Any more nominations? No? Okay then, let's vote. All in favor of appointing Harry Fische as CEO of the WCC, say aye."

My ears still hurt from that.

"All opposed?"

Two people yelled "NAY!" That was just about the only time the former Chief and I agreed on anything.

"The motion carries!" Meredith bounded up to the podium and grabbed my hand in her prosthetic one. She has a grip like Turk, and almost ripped my shoulder out of the socket pumping my arm up and down.

"The crabs aren't going to know what hit 'em, Harry," she said, grinning.

"I need a drink," I said, knowing it wouldn't really do me any good, but not knowing what else to say.

"I think that can be arranged." Meredith didn't even hit me for calling her Meri. I was amazed. "Why don't you call your whole crew in? I'd like Zook to talk to our engineers about that thing he popped in here and just how he did it."

"Uh, sure, Meredith." I keyed the comm and said, "Zook, you're never going to believe what just happened."

"I will make you a deal, Harry. I will believe you if you believe me."

"Huh? Yeah, okay." I figured he'd discovered something really interesting about the Sploig technology. "You first."

"I'm not going to be able to be your engineer for a while, Harry."

"What? Why not?"

"Well, because I'm going to be a father."

"What?" I was flabbergasted. The thought of Zook in *that* kind of a relationship made Kik's social life seem straight. "Who's the lucky girl?"

"Oh, there is no girl, Harry."

"Huh?" Did I mention flabbergasted?

"No girl, Harry. I'm going to have children."

"Huh? How?"

"Well, I'm not quite sure. You see, I've never been pregnant before, so I don't quite know how Immortals have children."

He lost me at the "P" word.

The human mind, prosthetic or organic, can only handle so many shocks before it needs some rest.

So that's why I'm here, and that's why you're buying me drinks. I'd tell you what happened next, but I see it's closing time. And since I've got a real job now, I better get back to the WCC.

Besides, I'm going to be an uncle. Or something like that.

Record # KR29387/β. Transcript ends.

Record # KR29387/β addendum:

Translation #1

Courtesy Encyclopedia Galactica, ten-thousand-four-hundred-twenty-fourth edition. © Intragalactic Press Inc.: This is a strange form of Earth Language (English) that is only encountered when large metallic objects are blocking the oropharynx of the speaker. Roughly "Gahh baaa ih ahh shuuu ih daau!" means "Get back in and shut it down!", but several points of inflection may have been lost in translation that indicate a certain urgency to the phrase.

I hope you are enjoying the Cheese Runner's Trilogy

Cheese Runners
Cheese Rustlers
Cheese Lords

Available in audio, electronic, and print formats

About the Author

From the sea to the stars, Chris A. Jackson's stories take you to the far reaches of the imagination. Raised on the back deck of a fishing boat and trained as a marine biologist, he became sidetracked by a career in biomedical research, but regained his heart and soul in 2009 when he and his wife Anne left the dock aboard the 45-foot sailboat *Mr Mac* to cruise the Caribbean and write fulltime.

With his nautical background, writing sea stories seemed inevitable for Chris. His acclaimed Scimitar Seas nautical fantasies won three consecutive Gold Medals in the *ForeWord Reviews* Book of the Year Awards. His Pathfinders Tales from Paizo Publishing combine high-seas combat and romance set in the award-winning world of the Pathfinder Roleplaying Game. Not to be outdone, Privateer Press released *Blood & Iron*, a swashbuckling novella set in the Iron Kingdoms.

Chris' repertoire also includes the award-winning and Kindle best-selling Weapon of Flesh Series, the contemporary urban fantasy *Dragon Dreams*, as well as additional fantasy novels, the humorous sci fi Cheese Runners trilogy of novellas, and numerous short stories.

To learn more, please visit jaxbooks.com.

Novels by Chris A. Jackson

From Jaxbooks
A Soul for Tsing
Deathmask

Weapon of Flesh Trilogy
Weapon of Flesh
Weapon of Blood
Weapon of Vengeance

Weapon of Flesh Trilogy II
(with Anne L. McMillen-Jackson)
Weapon of Fear
Weapon of Pain
Weapon of Mercy (summer 2017)

The Cornerstones Trilogy
(with Anne L. McMillen-Jackson)
Zellohar
Nekdukarr
Jundag

The Cheese Runners Trilogy
(novellas)
Cheese Runners
Cheese Rustlers
Cheese Lords

From Dragon Moon Press
Scimitar Moon
Scimitar Sun
Scimitar's Heir
Scimitar War